The Ayah and Other Stories

The Ayah and Other Stories

Chanis Fernando-Boisard

AMARYLLIS

AMARYLLIS

AMARYLLIS

An imprint of Manjul Publishing House Pvt. Ltd.

• 7/32, Ground Floor, Ansari Road, Daryaganj, New Delhi 110 002

Website: www.manjulindia.com

Registered Office:

10, Nishat Colony, Bhopal 462 003 - India

Distribution Centres:

Ahmedabad, Bengaluru, Bhopal, Kolkata, Chennai,
Hyderabad, Mumbai, New Delhi, Pune

ISBN 978-93-81506-81-3

This edition first published in 2017

Printed and bound in India by
Thomson Press (India) Ltd.

Contents

To my father Joseph Shelton Fernando,
28 March, 1925 – 20 July, 2016
...for the gift of words

A special thank you to my mother Yvonne,
to Alex,
and to my daughters

My thanks also go to Tanaka Mhishi, Lakshmi Mhishi,
Dawn Rodriguez, Janice Guinet
and to my sisters

Introduction

In *The Ayah and Other Stories,* expect the unexpected.

Chanis Boisard is a Sri Lankan writer living in Paris, whose amusing and thought provoking stories are superbly captured inspirations from her own life. Chanis explains that life is a cycle and one always keeps going back. In the first story, *The Ayah*, the central character Asilin's chilling warning about marrying a foreigner and the dangers of living overseas, is dramatically backed up by a lizard crying, which in Sri Lanka, is said to be a signal of foreboding and evil.

As a young girl Chanis, called Miss Nelun in the story, found this somewhat dramatic event deeply disturbing. But now, looking back with the wisdom of age, she realizes that Asilin had a point; one is best in one's homeland once that inner rebellion is done with. The power of this collection of stories is in the harsh realities of life's lessons that she succinctly sums up by saying, 'life is tough, life is unfair; why do some things happen to some and not to others, I wonder? Then I shrug my shoulders; what good does it do thinking? Let's just get on with what has to be done.'

For Chanis, jet-setting around the world in the airline travel business showed her how travel and tolerance go hand in hand...'the more people nurture prejudices, the more I scorn them.'

Like most Sri Lankans, this enigmatic and deeply spiritual writer is wary of the dangers of black magic and her superstitions are threaded throughout the book brilliantly, brought to life in *Living with the Huynhs*. 'From where I come, they say that hair is a perfect conduit for bad luck, spells and charms, which is why I have become so careful when cleaning my hairbrush or cutting my hair.'

Living overseas in the West has not changed her views on the spirit world as is highlighted in the chapter about a house she lived in... 'We who have lived in this house know that it conceals a hint of madness in its walls and corners. The bathtub on the first floor overflows for no good reason; in the basement pots of food burn to charcoal.' From an early age, Sri Lankan parents have their children's fingernails cut and burnt to stop them being used in spells to put on them.

Like the stories, Chanis has a femme fatale quality to her writing in which the expected ending is twisted, like in *The Ayah*, when she is told of Asilin's death on her wedding day. Instead of breaking down in tears, she quietly and firmly asserts: 'Will someone hand me the jasmines, please?'

I dare anyone reading this book not to shed a tear or two by the end of it. For Guillaume, in particular, who in the last story, one fears attended the football match at the Stade de France on that bloody Friday, 13th of November, one of France's worst terrorist incident's in 2015.

As the final pages of *The Ayah and Other Stories* were being edited, Chanis's father died suddenly and I asked her if this unexpected tragedy would trigger an early return to live once again in her home country... this quietly rebellious writer responded, 'I am not ready to go back.'

Juliet Coombe,
Publisher,
Sri Serendipity Publishing House,
Fort Galle, Sri Lanka

The Ayah

A lizard called from its corner. An air of uneasiness settled in the kitchen. The firelight picked out two figures. One had the bent appearance of an old woman, while the other's careless posture against the wall brought out her extreme youth.

The younger woman turned to face her companion and in a single word seemed to pose a question.

'So?' she asked.

The older woman spat out some betel with deliberation, and then shook her head.

'I still don't like it,' she said.

'But why, Asilin?' insisted the other. 'What have you got against him?'

Asilin, the older woman, spoke again: 'I don't have anything against him, but I know the ways of the world...yes, I do. I may be just an old servant, but I have seen life and seen plenty of these foreigners. There were hordes of them here during the war. If only you had seen those foreign soldiers and the way they behaved, you would never want to marry an outsider, Miss Nelun.'

'He is not a soldier, Asilin. You know that,' the girl, Nelun, interjected quickly.

'Yes, I know that,' answered Asilin. 'But, Missy, why don't you want to marry one of our own boys? Look at your mother now, and your aunts – they are happy, aren't they? Local girls should many local boys. You should have found a nice young Ceylonese boy. What about that young doctor who used to spend so much time here? Why not pick one of them and....'

Nelun broke into an impatient laugh. 'Ah, you can laugh,' continued the older woman, 'but Missy, I've worked with this family for three generations. I've seen your grandaunts and your aunts and then your cousins. They have all settled down quietly and happily with their own people. They bring their children here to see me and just like their mothers used to, these children too, sit in my kitchen and listen to my stories. But you Missy, of all people, the little one I've looked after...I never thought I'll live to see you marry a stranger and leave your home.'

Moved, the girl reached out and placed her hand on the old woman's bony shoulder. The ring she wore on her fourth finger touched Asilin's leathery skin for a moment. A strange fear possessed Asilin. Fear for this child, who meant more to her than even her own children. Questions tossed and turned in her mind like grains of rice being winnowed. They thumped in her brain with the dull insistence of a pestle thumping into a mortar. How would this young girl live so far away from everyone who was close to her? She was everyone's darling;

from Juanis, the old driver, to Banda, the mischievous young servant boy. How would she adjust to her new life? She had always lived a sheltered and cloistered life within the family circle up until now. And now here she was, casting away – as Asilin saw it – her entire life for a complete stranger. Would he treat her well? Would he always want her?

She began to speak again, as if to herself.

'I told myself that Miss Nelun is a sensible girl and knows what she is doing. She is her parents' only child and wouldn't do anything to displease them. I never thought this would happen...I can't believe it even now.'

She paused, but when she saw that Nelun had nothing to say to this, she spoke again, and this time directly to Nelun.

'Look Missy, you are no ordinary girl. Your father is the district judge. Everyone here knows him. I will not talk about the tea estates, which should be yours one day. Now, I do not know to whom they'll go. I just want you to remember that your parents have just you – and they are about to lose you.'

Asilin recognised the familiar expression of obstinacy that settled on Nelun's face. Seeing it, she started to speak gently, almost as if to a child. It seemed as though she was chiding Nelun for having been naughty.

In Nelun's mind, the years slipped back and she was a child again, being guided by her ayah. She saw Asilin run to pick her up as she rolled down the kitchen steps, she saw Asilin holding her hand at night when she was kept awake by scary memories of a ghost story she had read. She saw images of the two of them under an umbrella on a particularly rainy day, or of herself sitting goggle-eyed listening to Asilin's well-spiced, exaggerated tales. The screen in Nelun's mind focused on two tiny little hands knotted tightly round Asilin's neck, when she threatened to go away after having fought with old Juanis. Finally, the flashback came to rest on Asilin trying vainly to hide behind a scraggy guava tree in a game of hide and seek!

She shook her head vigorously as if to clear the cobwebs off her brain and tried to listen to the servant's words. It seemed as though she was once again in a classroom trying to concentrate on a lesson which she was not really interested in learning.

Asilin's concern for her well-being had affected her more than she would want to admit. She heard the old woman speak again, 'Missy, just think. This boy is lonely here in Ceylon; that's why he wants to marry you. What will happen when he goes back to his own country and is amongst his own people again? Will he still want you?

The unanswered question hung like suspended smoke in the silent kitchen and kept throbbing in Nelun's head. The darkness deepened, hiding their faces from each other.

To cover her uneasiness, Nelun made an attempt to change the subject.

'Come now, Asilin,' she pleaded with an attempt at gaiety. 'Just think of the nice things I'll send you from abroad. Think of how nice you'd look in those nylon saris. You'd look young again. I'll send you a nice black wig and you can then hide your grey hair. I'm sure Juanis will be on the kitchen steps again....you'll look so pretty!'

'What for,' snapped Asilin, 'Will all this be for my funeral?' Immediately regretting her thoughtlessness she said in a kinder tone: 'I don't want anything from you Missy. I only want you to be happy.'

'Don't worry. I will be happy. I am sure of that. I will let you know how I am faring. And when I have children, I shall bring them to see you. I'll tell them how you looked after me when I was a child.'

Asilin was slient. From some dark, hidden nook, the unseen lizard gave out its melancholy chirp again.* The old woman shivered slightly.

Tired of the tense silence, Nelun broke into Asilin's somber thoughts like a clumsy child eager to show off a new toy. 'Asilin!' she exclaimed, holding out her palm,'when I was younger you used to read my palm and tell me about the future. Tell me what is to come now. You told me before my last exam that I would do well and you were right. Tell me now what you foresee about my marriage?'

Asilin pressed her lips together firmly. 'No,' she replied, 'I am not a palmist. How can I predict anything? I shall leave it in the hands of the Buddha. He knows best what is good for you. I certainly do not. But you have my blessings. Now go and help your mother. She must be tired. She needs you.'

Two weeks later, Nelun sat at the mirror while the hairdresser combed out her hair. She was to wear it loose, with jasmines adorned on it.

A dozen people who thought themselves useful kept getting in her way. People, mechanical and robot-like, hurried around the room. Out in the yard, the women were playing the rabane.** The bridesmaids were giggling and anticipating the fun with delight. They minced about with awkward steps as they were still very young and were wearing a sari for the first time. Servants rushed about misinterpreting orders – generally causing confusion and consternation.

Nelun's parents moved about sad and anxious, but resigned and philosophical at the same time. They tried hard to look like a bride's parents should look, but the smiles kept sliding off their faces. They had learned their words, rehearsed their parts and they knew their cues. Now they blew words in different directions as they thought right and constantly kept correcting the downward twist of their mouths with a forced semblance of a smile.

But something was wrong. Or rather, everything seemed to be wrong. Someone whispered something in someone's ear, and soon there were busy whispers circulating around the room. Everyone spoke at the same time and everyone sought explanations. Then someone boldly demanded a confirmation. The bride's mother left the room to find out the truth. Someone nudged their neighbour and said that the bride must not know the sad news. The word passed round from one to another like a tasty morsel of food which they resolutely refused to share with Nelun. In the next few minutes, nothing remained in order. The hairdresser stopped, wielding her brush in mid-air, looking around, waiting for someone to enlighten her. Her curious screwed-up eyes analysed each person present in the room in turn. A row of blank faces stared back steadily at her, revealing nothing. The room seemed to be filled with people, but people that were like wooden carvings, looking down from the walls...onlookers to a crisis, a tragedy.

Nelun's mother entered the room. Her eyes caught her daughter's in the mirror and the sadness in them was reflected there. She began to speak to her daughter in a voice that was rather unsteady, yet somehow comforting.

'Nelun,' she began, 'I have some bad news for you...Asilin has passed away. She fell in the bathroom.'

She stopped, but when there was no response from her daughter, she continued, 'they said she looked rather peaceful lying there...almost happy.' She paused once again.

Everyone waited for Nelun to speak, to react. They all waited for some sign of grief, of Nelun having understood. They expected tears...bitter tears.

Nelun turned slightly. The tension in the air was palpable.

Then, quietly, she said: 'Will someone hand me the jasmines, please?'

*A lizard's cry is said to foretell evil.

**A *rabane* is a large drum placed on the floor, played by women in Sri Lanka on festive occasions.

The Story of a Smile

Yet another morning of lectures, Mr O'Neil announced that we had only a half-hour break for lunch and ignored the traditional groan. Once again we were to forgo one of those decent, hot meals from the University restaurant menu. Our minds were anchored at that period in time somewhere between 18th century England and contemporary American writing, with even 19th century French literature thrown in. Mr· Justin complimented me regularly on my creative writing but Mme Larriere chose to be a little harder, English to French translation she said, was still not of the required standard. Mr O'Neil always showed proof of a great sense of humour and tolerance, not only was I following his class on phonetics (learning to change my natural singsong accent to his standard pronunciation imitation of a poor British accent) he also was the Director of the Franco–Britannique university hall, where I resided.

By that period in time we were accustomed to pirouetting from the New Sorbonne down 13 Rue de Santeuil to Amplhi Richelieu at the old Sorbonne, situated at a certain distance from each other and sometimes even down Rue de L'École de Medicine, taking the Parisian metro, sandwich in hand. No. 6 Rue de L'École de Medicine was vastly popular, thanks to the Viennese bakery which used to be an old wartime haunt.

The end of the first term was fast approaching and we wondered if we had made the grade in continuous assessment, or if we would have to take the end of the year exams to be held in June. That feeling of nervousness seemed to be contagious. With strained faces at that time of the year and no energy for holiday plans, most of us could not even decide where to spend Christmas, obviously the most important point of the term.

It was one of those days, a cold winter morning when a bowl of soup would certainly have warmed us up. I stood in the queue of the cafeteria, resignedly, to collect my Quiche Lorraine comparing the prices as I usually did on my student budget. The sullen-faced girl in charge, approached me. I anticipated her usual rude reaction, her 'I don't care' attitude.

She handed me the quiche and for once her freckled face broke into a smile. Immediately I saw things in a different light. The pastries with a crack in the middle seemed to smile at me from their shelves, the eclairs with their chocolate coating gleamed, the apricot tarts beamed from their corner. I turned to go and on the exit staircase, I smiled at someone who bumped into me clumsily. He smiled at the lift-operator who grinned at the grey-haired teacher in her spectacles. Her severe features relaxed into the semblance of a smile when she met the pupil who got 5/20 on her last paper. She was so hopeful, thinking she had done well this time that she grinned at everyone in class and they all returned her smile. But when leaving, one of them smiled at the blind student whom we all helped and copied notes for – that stopped it all!

Lost and Found Secretary

As my father drove along the dusty roads of Mogadiscio, going from one airport office to another, to trace my lost suitcase, my mind went back to the events of the week before. We had not even said goodbye to each other, I could not help thinking of how empty that last week in Colombo had been. No amount of shopping for gifts to take for my classmates back in Paris, nor for my family in Africa nor the farewell dinners had helped to ease the pain of parting and not knowing what the future held for me.

We flew the Colombo-Seychelles stretch on a British Airways flight. My sister's baby slept peacefully in the hammock. On arrival in Seychelles, we were informed at the airport that my luggage had gone on to Cape Town, in South Africa, the final destination of the British Airways flight. The airline would make every effort to recover it, and send it back to me if I would only leave a forwarding address. All this sounded very convincing indeed.

The announcements of flights were made in Creole and we very nearly missed our flight from Seychelles to Mogadiscio. We arrived in Somalia, situated in the Horn of Africa on an Alitalia flight a few hours later. Our parents met us on arrival and commented on my appearance. They even wondered if I was sick! My father was then attached to the United Nations and our mail was delivered to PO box 24. I would insist that we go collect the mail, ever so often. To this day I'm still not sure what I hoped to hear at that time, that he wanted me back; was that it?

We cleared immigration and customs; jumping over a bench with a bunch of Somali immigration officers carefully observing the quality of the leap, indicated that one had actually been admitted into the country. The first impression of Somalia was of sand- coloured houses and mosques, regular reminders of prayertime; donkey-carts and robed women in the silent streets outside. Posters of Siad Barre, the President, adorned the walls. It was 1978 and Somalia and Ethiopia had a traditional border crisis which had lasted since 1942.

We were quick to make acquaintances with Mohammed the driver, who made our blue Fiat look very small, Mako the daily help, who performed folk dances on request and Aveez the night-watchman who would go home occasionally to his fourteen wives. Each time he left Mogadiscio, the temporary watcher would come and take up his post near the summer house, and the bush-babies would wander away. Furia, the Italian Alsatian dog, later to be promoted from our home to the Resident Representative's residence.

The next few days without my own clothes were a struggle. I strolled on the beach, met my Mum's friends at the sewing club; Solange, Hildegarde, Sue and all the others, young Jenny who sat at my mother's feet. Between Coffee mornings on the beach and lazy afternoons in the company of the Egyptian Ambassador's three daughters, the days flew by. Occasionally on an evening I would taste the lobster dinner at Azans – that too – dressed in my younger sister's ill-fitting skirts and tops. I managed to convince my father, that I was lacking essential clothing. I suggested trying the Mogadiscio open market, where everything was available from clothes to smoked camel milk and Somali pastry stands. This saved me from miming to curious, giggling vendors. I spoke neither Somali nor Italian!

Our visits to the airport were of no avail. A board read 'Lost and Found Secretary,' a display that sent my younger sister and myself into a fit of giggles. An encouraging 'the baggage should reach in the course of the next week, Insh'Allah' would be thrown at us before the employee got up and wandered away lethargically.

Sometimes it would be prayertime and we would wait patiently. They spoke a mixture of English and Somali, rather guttural in sound. One would think they were very angry but it was just the tone they used.

A friend of my parents working as a pilot at PIA allowed himself to be persuaded to intervene at this stage. Just a few telephone calls, telexes and through his personal contacts at British Airways, we were now informed that the luggage would arrive in Mogadiscio the next day, as simple as that.

The next day, once the post flight formalities were done with, we followed the official to the Lost and Found Secretary's office. I went ahead of the others, excited about finally getting my suitcase after one week of survival without it. In his dusty little office there was baggage of all kinds and shapes, Delseys and Visas, those held together by a plastic cover, those tied up with rope so as not to fall apart.

Standing alone proudly was mine, tied up with a red ribbon. I recognised my name written in my familiar scrawl, and approached it with alacrity. My sister, Peter and Simon stood by. The official wiped his spectacles and touched his forehead wearily. We had seen him almost every day. I took out the key and fitted it in. The suitcase fell open. I searched for my swimsuit bought for Mogadiscio beach, my one and only evening dress and my stack of letters. I recognised nothing. There was some skimpy, masculine clothing and a few magazines. Even in my immense disappointment, I noticed the lost and found secretary now beating a hasty retreat.

Letter to Nelun

My dear Nelun,

Thank you for your last letter, I've taken the time to reply since I wanted to think over everything you said. I've noticed that you've deliberately avoided commenting on what is commonly termed as 'my summer romance.' You are no doubt surprised as in one letter I sounded rapturously happy and I told you I was practically engaged to the guy you knew me to be in love with for the last three years – and in the next you witnessed the end of an affair, the standard comments and the dull regrets.

I'll try to explain it: To begin with it wasn't simply a summer romance. We'd known each other for ages and trusting him was only natural. I've described him to you. You know everything about him: every gesture, his walk, his smile, so I need not go through it again.

One thing I have to admit is that I had closed my eyes to the possible change that could take place within a separation of a certain period of time. The person I left behind had not yet learned to swear, he was practically a boy – and the one I discovered this summer was a different person altogether, very bothered about keeping up his male image!

Our first few weeks together were, in short, very happy. There was little to spoil it, we had no obstacles, no apparent parental opposition. We spoke about the future, about what we would do when I returned. The days passed filled with trivial amusements, shared jokes and moments together. An unexpected visitor was always a hindrance and we always contrived to get rid of him, laughing over our success later in the evening. Besides our relationship was a secret between us and a few trusted friends (like yourself) and we always enjoyed pretending especially in company where sometimes we hardly ever spoke to each other. It was, you could say, a charade.

Then as it drew closer to my departure, a change set in. I sensed at times that something had changed, although it was not to point one's finger to it; my questioning was futile. I realised that he understood only then the full responsibility of a relationship, and he found he was too young to commit himself. I search for excuses but although months have passed, I still find it difficult.

So he began to pick an argument whenever he could. He never lost his temper but he was sullen and moody and gradually the whole glamour of the relationship went out. Meanwhile I became more possessive, I tried to be a dozen people at once since I was not sure which one he wanted! So every evening when he came it was as if he drew lots and picked out a different me. Our last few evenings were a pretence on his side and an attempt on mine. We were merely trying to keep alive something which had burnt itself out. Or was it something that never existed?

It did not even end with a quarrel which is ironic, just an issue of one not giving into the other's will and he was very quick to make use of the situation and it ended there. So for you who always say things should be ended gracefully, we didn't even say goodbye!

And so it became in the eyes of the world just another summer romance, still another story of a girl picking up someone for her temporary amusement. I wonder what they say of him? You know I never meant it that way!

I think I've told you everything. I hesitated at first but I know you so well, you would have puzzled over it in your mind. I am certain you would say with that smile of yours that acceptance is the very essence of maturity.

You would be right anyway if you do say so, maturity comes to us all. Autumn has a particularly soothing quality. Besides in its quietness there is a certain repose if you look for it. The colours of autumn are a symbol of that maturity; we watch the leaves fall and in spring we'll watch the trees re-leaving.

Spring is such a long time away after the cold and hardship of winter. Who knows what the spring brings? On this note I end.

Mystery in Mogadiscio

I had just arrived in Mogadiscio for the second time and was in a different frame of mind from the year before. Things went more harmoniously; even my straw hat, bought from Lakpahana, the tourist shop in Colombo, had followed me intact from Paris to Mogadiscio, via Barcelona. My sister's guardian in the UK, Mrs Gomez, had sent me a special present. Not only was she my sister's guardian, she was also my mentor.

With her natural optimism, Mrs Gomez had sent a blank recipe book for me to fill in with my culinary experiments during my travels in Spain and Somalia. She had witnessed my pathetic efforts to turn out stir fried potatoes, ala thel dala, Sri Lankan style, that first Christmas in Wimbledon. She had decided that after familiarising me with Chaucer and Shakespeare, she was going to make a decent cook out of me!

Never having studied Spanish during my schooldays in Colombo, I would sit down in the evenings to prepare for the next batch of exams. While the meshed windows kept the malaria mosquitos at bay, Kenyan tea helped me to study late into the night and to chat with my sister.

Just as my parents returned from their annual 'rest and recuperation' leave in Nairobi, the first disappearance within the diplomatic circle took place. Because of the backdrop of the war and the possibility of kidnappings, the expatriates hardly stepped out of the strictly defined borders of the capital, Mogadiscio.

Word got around that a special requiem service was to be held for the deceased Mr Marks. Lost at sea, or so they said, supposedly gobbled up by sharks. Thread and knitting needles in hand, a lot of gossip was exchanged at the morning sewing sessions. The ladies' imagination ran so wild, they could have easily put Hercule Poirot to shame!

Sister Emmanuella decided to restore some order. She summoned everyone for choir practice and invited Monseigneur Francisco to say mass. My mum gave up her voluntary task of icing cakes for christenings, while Kate, Pat and Sue left their unfinished sewing, quite relieved.

Other welfare associations and UN volunteers hastened for practices. Störğ, the Finnish librarian, was persuaded to sing the Ave Maria. The Egyptian and Indian Ambassadors' wives stood by for moral support. For a while, nothing mattered except making a success of Mr Mark's final journey, so much so that even the bridge players abandoned clubs, hearts and spades to join in the preparations.

The service was over but a strange aura of uncertainty remained; a feeling of doubt. Had Mr Marks really been eaten by a shark? Enemy boats constantly approached Somali waters. Suspicion remained in that little, secluded diplomatic community about his disappearance. Inquiries continued to be made as to what could have become of him. A close watch was kept on locals hired as cooks, drivers and watchmen. Social workers were roped in. Some even considered hiring a detective. Embassies pressed upon their personnel to exercise caution. Return home before dark, they warned.

Maco, our cook, would leave earlier, while Mariam, the maid would stay on longer with us during those troubled days. Every day, Maco would prepare a green pepper, zucchini and tomato salad and leave the lamb casserole at a safe height, out of our dog Furia's reach. She would then wrap her Somali shawl of delicate, green muslin around her head and make a dash for the gate, trying not to attract Furia's attention. A dance-like ritual followed, where half in anger and half in jest, Maco would cry out in her attempts to extricate herself from the dog's paws; Once outside our premises, she would quicken her step as her bare feet touched the hot sand and cast a furtive glance around.

We were to leave Mogadiscio on 12th September. As the day drew close, Mariam performed tribal dances like someone in a trance, while Furia kept time with her tail. She sometimes gazed at us with eyes like limpid pools, somehow sensing our imminent departure. Time seemed measured by the muezzin's daily calls for prayers, at dawn and dusk and in between.

Aeroplanes constantly flew over our house in Kilometre 7, on their way to land at the airport. Once again we would walk through the desert sands to collect extra saucepans from the McDonald family for the farewell party...little did anyone suspect that the last 'nuisance call' to order McBurgers from McDonalds had come from my sister and me on an idle Somali afternoon!

Then, just a few days before were to return to Europe, Aveez, our night watchman was called back home. One of his fourteen wives was seriously ill. Before he left, he made arrangements for the temporary watchman Farook to stand in for him. This was hardly good news for us. Not only could Farook not communicate in English, the bushbabies just seemed to disappear when he approached!

Mariam the maid, my sister and I would be in-charge of the house during my parent's evening engagements, while Farook was responsible for the compound outside. I continued to learn my verbs when I was not writing to my friends at university in Paris. My sister would try out recipes learnt at her boarding school in England: Haddock Kedgeree, pizza, all British style. The rest of the time, she would play squash against our high, secluded garden wall.

It was not a surprise that Mariam and Farook would argue everyday. Their voices often raised to a Somali crescendo, could be heard over the din of the radio which we kept on just to create a presence...to convey to those outside that there were people in the house.

Then, one evening, alarmed by a sudden scream, I threw down my book of verbs and hurried out to the summer house. My sister followed closely behind with her squash racket, as if for protection.

'What's going on Mariam?' I demanded, casting aside thorny bougainvillea branches to approach her. I could not communicate with Farook. He looked away when spoken to. Mariam was reticent to talk. Her eyes were round and intent. Her hands trembled as she spread them out towards us.

'But what is it, Mariam?' I cried. She turned unwillingly towards the watchman. Her body heavy, she interrogated him and translated his answers for us, sentence by sentence, her voice shrill and unrecognisable. She was never like this in front of my parents.

Farook towered over us, dominating, sure of himself. He informed Mariam that Mr Marks was a spy! No one spoke after Mariam translated his words. Then I asked Mariam what made him say that. What proof did he have? I tried to appear cold and clinical. I would not let him take the upper hand. Farook withdrew to a corner and gazed at the full moon. His arms outstretched, he moaned and beat his chest. Although I could not understand the language, I knew what the gesture meant.

'Allah forgive me.'

No one spoke. Mariam was shaking. I placed my arm gently around her shoulders. Farook went on to reveal that Mr Marks had been beheaded by a rival gang, and then thrown into the sea, very close to the beach hut. For a minute we could say nothing. Far away, we heard Furia utter a baleful moan.

'How does he know all this?' my voice was subdued.

I felt very uneasy. Mariam repeated my question to Farook in Somali. He said nothing. He wrote something on the sand from right to left. Awed, Mariam knelt down to read what he had written. The garden light picked out the letters drawn in the heap of sand. Furia howled again in a long, melancholy moan, a chilling sound that I had never heard in my twenty-two years.

'Please Mariam, tell us what he has written?' Mariam seemed pensive, distant like a stranger. I felt the weight of the situation, being responsible for the house and for my sister, until our parents returned around midnight.

No one spoke. I challenged Farook with a bold stare. He must not sense the fear I felt.

'Missy, I used to work in his house,' the watchman replied in English, slowly and deliberately.

I took a few steps backwards, caught completely off balance.

He noticed my astonishment at hearing him articulate in perfect English. A strange smile twisted his face.

'I saw it all happen,' he said, his eyes gleaming in the dark....

The German Master's Wife

'I'm awfully sorry,' he repeated 'terribly sorry.' Are you really sure you want me to come over? I mean, are you sure it won't disturb you at this particular time?'

'No,' repeated the other,' 'In fact, I'd be happy if you came, really.'

His words seemed sincere enough to convince the pupil. Maybe his master meant it. He could be even lonely. 'I'll be there.' He said, a little gruffly, so as not to show his sympathy too much. 'I'll be there at 06:30 PM.'

At 6:20 PM, the pupil presented himself at the German master's house. The master met him at the door. His face was very much as usual, a slight moustache and beard which had begun to sprout being the only difference.

'Come in,' he said. Eric followed him, his helmet in his hand, his clean-scrubbed face, the face of a choirboy gleaming in the light. He took the place indicated to him. A black cat jumped onto the table and continued to climb airily till she was perched on the propped-up mattress, basking under the light of the study lamp. She disregarded Eric completely, as usual.

'Like some tea?' asked the German master. 'Yes, of course,' Eric replied mechanically. The master always offered him tea and he replied through politeness. Personally, he preferred coffee.

His master went into the kitchen. One could hear him, banging saucepans about and a little later he emerged, holding the familiar little clay teapot, and two cups. Suddenly as the master was pouring out the tea, Eric remembered how it had been at other times. Usually if was the German master's wife, who poured the tea, dressed in some exotic costume, meeting his eyes occasionally, her hands trembling over the teapot and meeting his eyes in a shy kind of way.

They started the lesson. Eric conjugated his verbs, showed the last week's translation and got it corrected. It struck him that the master was somewhat distracted; he hadn't noticed some obvious faults. But then, in the circumstances, Eric told himself.

As they continued the master felt the need for the grammar book, to explain something better, he said. He got up, went to the other room and groped around in the half-light. He returned presently, somewhat perplexed.

'I can't find it. I really don't know where she put it after the last lesson.'

'It doesn't matter,' Eric said, 'maybe we could do another translation.'

The master seemed not to have heard what he said; 'I don't understand it,' he said, 'nothing is in its proper place, what got into her?'

'Maybe she didn't know what she was doing,' said Eric cautiously. It was the first time that he had dared refer to the German master's wife.

'Oh, she did, she did alright,' replied the other emphatically. 'She foresaw it a long time ago, she prepared herself for it.'

Eric said nothing. Suddenly it seemed to him that there was nothing to say. His role of questioner, interrogator had suddenly changed into the role of a listener, voluntary or not.

'She spoke to me about it so many times. She was obsessed by it,' continued the other musingly, 'it seemed to her, to be her only way out.'

Suddenly aware of Eric, he paused. 'You can't understand it, can you? It's difficult for me too at my age. But I don't blame her. I never will. What good would it do?'

The hour ticked away. Eric suddenly felt, on listening to the teacher, that he understood the grown-up world better; their way of thinking, of loving, of forgiving the unforgivable. He wondered what his own life would be like and he hoped it would always be simple and secure like that of his goldfish in its little, round, glass bowl.

The hour was over. A little cry from the other room could be heard, that of a little baby, unaware of the changes in the adult world, demanding to be fed, it asked just that its hunger be satisfied.

The master made a move as if to get up. His eyes were unseeing as he looked before him. Eric pushed his 50 franc note before him, on the table. The master accepted it absently, knowing that once Eric had gone through the door, the loneliness would begin again, the thousands of tomorrows, which lay ahead of him and which he would have to live.

The Baby-Minder

'What awful weather,' she exclaimed as she came in, shaking the water off her raincoat as if to indicate that she had been through a storm. 'Such a terrible month of March!' I nodded mechanically as I checked my purse to see if I had enough money to pay her on my return, telling myself that she always tended to exaggerate a little.

'The feed is ready.' I said, 'She shouldn't wake up till 11 AM. Don't worry about her cold. She's much better than the last time.' I put on my boots, buttoned my coat and made for the door. 'Well,' I said, 'see you at twelve then.' I returned earlier than usual. The lecture was boring. Mme Bourcier was absent and the lecturer who stood in for her was not able to capture our attention through 17th century England, nor could she touch on the subject of children's literature in the same way that Mme Bourcier did. The language exchange that had started off with great enthusiasm with Anne K was not going to take place either and besides, the babysitter was new, my mind was not really at ease. Transport was on time and I reached the little suburb in which I lived, in no time....

I stepped off the bus and climbed up the slope that led to my flat. I stopped to say 'hello' to one of my neighbours. She told me her rheumatism was just as bad and asked if the baby was alright. I could feel the indirect accusation. I could guess what was going on in her head. 'Her baby is not even two months old and here she is running around. I assured her that the baby was alright, said goodbye for the third time, finally got to my flat, where I rang the bell feeling slightly tense with anticipation.

There was no answer. I rang once more giving her time to finish whatever she was doing and come to the door. No one replied. I supposed she had the baby in her arms and could not reach the door in time. I rang for a third and final time. There was still no response. I unlocked the door, secretly relieved that I always kept a spare key with me.

A half-finished baby bottle was left on the table. There was no one in the sitting room or in the kitchen. There was no one in the dining room either. I made my way to the bed room. The baby lay where I left her in the morning, unaware of any change around her. Her soft toys, the little pink mouse and the grey hedgehog kept her company.

Her rattle and her little pink cotton mouse lay beside her silently and the only sound I could hear, as I bent over her to reassure myself, was that of her breathing.

The Snake

There had never been much affection between the two women. They were not made to understand each other. The elder one was a perfectionist and intolerant of everyone else's faults. The younger one was clumsy and generous and always ready to receive whatever scraps of affection one bestowed on her, gladly. In her efforts to be loved, she reminded the older woman of the door she had shut upon her; one she felt she couldn't unlock. She wondered why she felt that way but she just could not help herself. One has no control of one's sentiments or emotions, she thought.

In a fit of anger, the elder woman called the younger one a snake because of her long lithe movements, and most of all because of the little head posed on a long neck, as also because of everything else; the nostrils and the eternal look of incomprehension. That look irritated the elder woman most. She wanted to give her affection, but couldn't. Something held her back. It was almost as if the younger woman said that she was not capable of seeing anyone else happy. Was that true, she wondered?

Then one day, the younger woman disappeared, leaving no trace and the older one continued to live, lonely at times, and set in her ways, changing nothing in her clockwork existence.

One hot afternoon, she felt a movement in the garden as she sat there thinking. The insects all scurried away. Lifting her head she saw a snake, its body pasted against the wall and its head hanging down. When it did lift its head, it was that of the younger woman.

Astonished, she moved back, but the snake stayed in its position never once looking away. Its expression was so intense, so questioning, that the woman could not shift her own gaze away. She stared, mesmerized. She wondered who the snake reminded her of; she almost recognised a familiar look of reproach. The woman trembled slightly; she questioned herself on the past, wondered what she had done to receive these visits that made her so uneasy. From that day onwards, the snake came back, again and again. It never approached her…but just passed by.

At Farida's Post

I sit here at Farida's post. It's still another austere, gloomy morning in mid-January, since she left and abandoned her tasks to me. No light, no sunshine, sipping cold tea not coffee, slipping into her place, into her skin. Gloomy, sullen, lack of enthusiasm, cold and superior, dreams of travel, of escape, of other places. Dressed in uniform, not in black – but that hardly seemed to brighten up anything. Not the office, the prospects nor the mood.

Here I am, taking on still another file, acting the way she did, thinking like her, almost aping her behaviour. Her impatience with some, her preference for those of Latin kind, her moods and feelings becoming mine, gradually.

The rhythm changes. I don't go at the same pace; I don't breathe the same way ; I can't go so fast, my pace slows down. I'm not into the same things. No iPod on my ears to know what's happening outside, to listen to the world news or to learn about the latest bomb blast. Not as yet, that's still not me.

Just before work, listening to soothing opera music, Maria Callas, Sergio's comforting voice on the Italian radio. That's me, not Farida. Dreaming of better days and thinking of things the way they used to be. Life is tough, life is unfair; why do some things happen to some and not to others I wonder? Then I shrug my shoulders; what good does it do thinking? Let's just get on with what has to be done.

As I go on, doing her work, doing mine, merging into her existence, remaining me, becoming her. Her computer sometimes doesn't function, sensing her absence, feeling my touch on the keys. Her phone sometimes doesn't work either. Her agents don't want me around except when they are hopelessly stuck. 'She did it this way,' they tell me. 'Not like that.' 'She did it better, she did it faster, better than you.'

Black blotches fall from my pen. I get up. I've had enough for the day. I go to the ladies' room, stare at myself in the mirror hoping no one would come in, and see me in my red jacket, discontented, lips drooping down. Another sleepless night, body cold with the previous day's glasses of red wine, remembering her tremble after the wine. Was that me, was it her?

I honestly don't know.

Till Tomorrow

'Something terrible is happening to my eye,' she heard him say and she felt something icy cold gripping her tight. 'I've called Dr Hoem. He insists that I see a specialist urgently,' he continued.

During the next few weeks, they lived from consultation to consultation, from Tuesday to Tuesday; from soup to soup. New hopes raised, only to be dashed again. The doctors all advised him to wait, just wait for it to subside. They promised laser treatment, they promised operations, a second opinion with a famous specialist. But everything they said was punctuated by 'if'...if the haemorrhage subsided. At the same time she pondered whether he would be able to work again, would they be able to complete the payments on the house?

The Friday preceding Easter, he observed something very dark rising from the bottom of his eye. He called her immediately. She tried every number at the eye hospital. She called every service, but it was a Friday and she knew the French traditionally had weekend fever and the best specialists would be away in their villas in Cannes or wherever. He thought it best to rush to the emergency service without waiting for her, bumping into people and getting gently rebuked. It seemed like hours before it was 5 and she was free to finally join him. The pain and fear in his voice haunt her still. By that time, the doctors at the emergency service had decided that there was no alternative but to operate the very next day.

'You are part of his family, aren't you? Maybe you could go home and collect his things?' the doctor told her abruptly, between pre-operation blood tests and ECTs. Considering how late it was, there was no point returning, to get his things for one night. She stayed as long as she could, braving the nurse's disapproval. She adjusted his light, shared his dinner and got back home, sleeping for the first time alone, in that empty house that they had only occupied for 29 days.

The next day, she packed his clothes carefully, his slippers (she had seen his bare feet on the cold, tiled floors at the hospital), his vests and a dressing gown. She could hardly afford to buy him a new pair of pyjamas. They were going through patch of financial difficulty, until they sold their flat, in order to pay for the new house. She could not help feeling the weight of every expense. His room was empty when she reached the hospital. The sheets had been removed. She panicked, rushed till the end of the corridor till she met the Sister, nurse in charge. 'He's just gone for his Betadine bath, he'll be back soon,' she said kindly.

A nurse entered, left the sedative carelessly on the bedside, gave her scrappy instructions to be conveyed to her husband as she was due to be off-duty. She remained in the room till he was taken into the operation theatre. She then sat on the bench outside, her fingers glued to the rosary but not moving. She must have been there from 2.45 to 7.15 PM, refusing to leave the hospital till she actually saw him wheeled back to the room.

During the next few weeks, there was some hope of him regaining sight in the weak eye. He would suddenly say 'you look nice in that black coat today.' Her heart would lift, and she would smile, pleased at the progress he was making. But a fresh detachment of the retina followed and this time something went wrong in the operating theatre. For what was to be months, he could visualise the scalpel approaching his eye during the operation, he pictured the surgeon in his blue robes, bending over him. He saw the attendants in green robes. He seemed to hear a short discussion, the hushed murmuring and then a minute of silence, when something unexpected took place.

A few days after the operation and once he discovered he did not see any more, the surgeon and his staff would not see them. Telephone calls were filtered, the door was locked, and no explanations were given. When he was discharged, he pretended to be cheerful so as to ease her pain, while waiting for things to get better – if they did get better. He sat in front of the computer, seeing little. He took up a newspaper only to lay it aside. He sat at the wheel but couldn't drive. His silence was eloquent; she knew him so well. Everything that looked so black for him was reflected in the dejection and darkness of her soul. She woke up long before 6 AM ever so often, crawled exhausted to work. She went from day-to-day and week by week wondering whether one day, his sight would improve.

Would he ever see her the way he used to?

Living with the Huyhns

We moved to our new house in February 2009, on Friday the 13th. We should've known better. You just don't move into a new home on such an inauspicious date!

Never could we have imagined what we were to go through here. On the day we moved in all my cooking efforts to prepare a mouth-watering Rendang, an Indonesian specialty with citronella and spice scents infusing the atmosphere were lost on everyone. The reminder of good Asian cooking, which came straight from Priya Wickremasinghe's cookbook, went totally unnoticed.

Mr Huyhn oozed charm from every pore from the very moment we met him. Now that I think of it, he was almost servile. But then, we were probably the only people impulsive enough to buy his beautiful yet threatening house. I remember the day we met him as if it were yesterday. I even remember what I was wearing, a grey top and a long skirt which I had bought in Paris. In my frenzy to find a new house, I had spent a whole year scouring the Internet for the perfect place. With the budget we had, it wasn't easy to find the place I wanted. It had to be in the near suburbs, close to the express train station, and Gentilly was just right. Nitya, my daughter laughed at me. She knew that I had set my heart on Huyhn's house from the very beginning.

Finding the perfect house became an obsession for us both although it never came to the point of keeping me awake at night. We were both growing older, and soon the banks would no longer be willing to grant us a loan. I told myself that time passing by allowed us save more. In the meantime, I applied for hotel reception jobs, offered to provide private tuition and even tried my luck at games, but nothing came up. I finally approached a famous jeweller down Rue de la Paix in Paris to sell a pendant given to me at birth by my a late aunt, but it was not a genuine sapphire We argued about the house. My husband felt fine about living far away from public transport while I did not. I was very careful and took every precaution to make sure that we both thought the same thing, that we agreed in our disagreement.

It was in September last year when we visited this house for the first time. Mr. Huyhn and son were busy doing up the garden. We could see them through the glass door at the back of the house. He was very polite, ever so happy to show his unexpected visitors around the house. He shared travel experiences; told us about his transfer to Singapore, about his present position in a prestigious firm. We were totally under the charm. I had always thought that my husband was the naïve one, but I too was completely caught in the beautiful web that was being spun around us, a little more skilfully at each encounter.

Climbing up the staircase, we marvelled at the mezzanine, we went crazy over the garden and admired the black Buddha statue perched in a niche in what became our bedroom window. We imagined an old Vietnamese grandmother, hair tied back in a chignon, climbing up the staircase every night, while her young student boarders slept in the basement. We could visualise it all. We didn't know then that it was a house...

Today we, who have lived in this house know that it conceals a hint of madness in its walls and corners. The bathtub on the first floor overflows for no good reason, in the basement pots of food burn to charcoal. In vain I scratched and dug the garden soil to find a clue to the spell which haunted the house, but all I found were scraps of metal. I even overturned the pot of artificial Hydrangeas to reveal only slugs and snails feasting on cabbage and mutilating strawberries so lovingly tended. I never found the culprit charm.

From where I come, they say that hair is a perfect conduit for bad luck, spells and charms, which is why I have become so careful when cleaning my hairbrush or cutting my hair. The Huyhns too came from Asia. I believe that they held the same beliefs and fears. Their knowledge on this subject was surely greater than mine. Each time I bent over the strawberry patch, I could feel my hair being caught by rose thorns. The blue toilet door opened by itself more often than not. Exchanging glances we tried to convince one another that it was just a draft. I heard water running upstairs at night, but my husband heard nothing, even straining his ears to listen. I would insist and tell him that old Mrs Huyhn must be running a bath.

The Huyhns were there, I sensed them everywhere when I closed the door at night, when I approached the lonely bathroom window to look out at our neighbour's barren fig tree. They had never really left us. Their tools still lay in the garden shed. After the sale of their house they had dropped by and left us some more hanging flower pots, filled with greyish earth forming little circle-like eyes, little round eyes watching us and waiting...for what? For us to leave? For them to return to recover something which they left behind? The four white chairs which we left outside seemed to draw closer to each other at night, as if someone had been sitting on them, as if secret meetings went on there at night. A gaunt, pony-tailed student called Lee stayed with us for 6 months. She lived on egg and cucumber soup and I'm sure that she had a sense of foreboding when she left our house for good.

Once, I fell upon some photos that our elder daughter Ranya had taken of the house on one memorable 26th October – the day after our wedding anniversary. It was the day on which the six of us had visited the house, escorted by Mr Huyhn. There was one photo of Nitya and of her boyfriend on the staircase, and one of us all in the garden. When I look back now at what we've been through since, I fear for others...

I'm not sure it is of any use, but I finally abandoned that pot of Hydrangeas in a far away church, as a talisman to keep the Huyhns at bay.

The Moon Sisters

We were both standing behind the ticket counter, bent over a fare calculation, eyebrows wrinkled in deep concentration, was it a circle trip, a half-around-the-world? Strange how she looked at me at times, as if wondering about something. There was something very attractive about her attitude, gestures, about her hands moving like those of a dancer. She used to play the piano as a child, and hummed a tune eternally. She did not know though, that I played the classical guitar. I had never told her. Stay reserved at work, I had always told myself. Stay outwardly friendly, a good conversationalist, but reveal nothing of the inner hurt, the inner pain that life invariably inflicts.

We had worked with each other for over a year now, and it was time for me to leave for a vacation. As usual, I could not make up my mind about where to go.

'Go to Israel,' she suggested, 'you'll love it there. Besides, there is my cousin's flat you could use.'

I hesitated, thinking of everything we heard on the news about Israel.

'Well, there aren't more bombs there than where you come from,' she teased. The idea of staying in a kibboutz at least for a few day really appealed to me.

'You had better let me know in advance,' she encouraged me, 'Yom Kippour is not far and I'll certainly be taking a few days off.'

'I'm not sure they will give you leave this time,' I said tactfully, trying to prepare her, aware that I was treading on slippery ground. 'It's the high season, they need us here.'

She was taking leave anyway, she replied firmly, however the management might take it. I sighed, knowing that though her personality could often carry the day for her, during high season, the management had its own way of dealing with things. I did not wish to get into trouble because of her whims and fancies.

I was relieved when a passenger walked in, giving me the opportunity to move on to something else. She offered to handle him which suited me just fine. I could not help wondering what made her the way she was: whimsical, secure and high spirited. She had certainly had a very different upbringing to mine. I hardly knew what it was to be lavish, having always had to share with my sisters; we had had a strict education, rather like in a boarding school or even the army, with a time and place for everything. She just showered boxes of chocolates on the rest of us, carried bottles of jam from her husband's hometown, took me out to a restaurant on my birthday and to crown it all, gifted me with an enormous hamper from Marks & Spencer for Easter.

She respected my religion, never scoffing if I was at church during lunchtime. I would listen with fascination when she spoke about her visits to the synagogue on Saturdays and the Yom Kippur tradition.

I was grateful when she stood in for me at very short notice during my trip to Nepal and then again in the summer, when I took a holiday with my two girls. I reciprocated by handling her tour operators, which meant checking endless lists of names over and over again; marked in pink for the wait-listed passengers and blue for those with confirmed bookings.

Ironically, on Christmas Eve, she would choose to go home early and I would stay on ensuring that everything was in order for the next day's flight departures. I would call home to give instructions on the roast, the potatoes and the decor. I would rush to take the suburban train, arriving just in time to get changed into my evening dress before the guests started arriving with Christmas presents.

Strangely, she proved to be very superstitious. I learnt that she had actually read tea leaves before joining the company. She claimed she had seen us all before, and even knew the sound of my voice! She had seen visions of the flight register, each flight being placed in a file in order of date. I could scarcely believe her; how could she have seen us before she actually joined us?

Towards the end of the day, done with our accounts and having put the tickets back into the safe, we both stood there with the evening sun catching our red uniforms, one fair and with curly hair bunched up in some kind of pony tail and the other with her typical South Asian appearance. But we both had the same hands, one's perfumed, the other's not. I wondered about this resemblance between us, especially in gesture – the way we leant over the desk, the way we ran a hand through our hair absent-mindedly, humming a tune when no passenger was in sight. Strangely enough, we both would often choose the same tune!

'Did you know it?' she asked breaking into my musings 'Did you know about us?'

'What about us?' I asked, thinking vaguely that she must have gotten too much sun.

'Did you ever stop to think about the conferences your father attended in Israel?' she went on.

I was rather bewildered, not sure what she was getting at.

'Because,' she continued, now almost laughing that silly laugh she had at times, 'because he was my father too.'

'Sarah,' I exclaimed angrily, 'you must be crazy. How can you say such a thing?'

Then, during the short silence that followed, it all came back to me: how she had rushed to apply for the job, how she'd phone me almost everyday ever since the advertisement came out!

'My dear,' her tone was firmer, a little condescending, 'the photo you showed me when I came over to your home...'

'Yes, what about it?' I snapped.

'Well, my mother has that photo too,' her tone was emphatic.

'Doesn't mean a thing, anyone could get a photo of him, he was in the news so often.' My voice was unsteady. I was losing ground. I caught myself peering at her through eyes like slits, a trifle dizzy. Suddenly, it seemed so warm at the counter...had she left the radiator on again?

'Think what you like, believe what you wish.'

She had taken on that stubborn, satisfied look – of the cat that got the cream – but there was also a softness now, the comfort and sureness of one who knows.

'My mum says that we are Moon Sisters.'

Grandma's Gelatine Bowl

Crates of Agapanthus from the hill country of Nuwara Eliya adorned the passageways in bow-shaped baskets, a traditional reminder of St John's feast, Mutwal. Their scent invaded the huge, sprawling house. The whirring of the Kenwood beater; puddings and soufflés being prepared...this is what I remember of that particular day. The grown-ups had decided it was my turn to beat the gelatine in yet another of my grandmother's numerous bowls. Containers and saucepans adorned the wall, and Perera would fetch drinking water from the ceramic filter. Sometimes, Jonas would take over from him, when it was one of his 'good' days.

I must have been pretty young. I was wearing my dark green and white spotted pinafore, which I had also worn for my sixth birthday in the family holiday home, Claremont, up in the hill-country where the family met in the Nuwara Eliya 'season' every April.

I missed the fat kitchen Amme's story of Lourdes this time. It was always the same one: how Bernadette had dipped her feet in the water and had been cured forever. When you're very young and the whole adult world wants you out of sight and out of mind on a hot summer afternoon, you stay quietly in bed, listening to stories and you believe anything under the sun that is told to you. That's how it was for me, too.

My mother's sisters were everywhere, their conversation animated. They had so much in common with one another and yet, were so different. From serious Noeline to giggling Shirla and charming Cynthia to shy Myrna. My mother and my godmother Loku Amma usually struck a contrast to the others – you could say that they were more of an advisory commitee!

I started beating the gelatine with enthusiasm, at first feeling a little important at being singled out for the task, listening to my aunts' chatter punctuated by advice from the kitchen Ammas. I continued beating till my hand was very sore and I was bored. Meanwhile, my cousins noisily explored the bedroom drawers and other curious nooks and crannies. They may even have found labels of fruits – my grandfather was a ship chandler and he had labels of all kind to distinguish one food item from another, like those for peach and cherry. We were all very much at the scrapbook stage at that age of six or seven, and I envied them, thinking of my scrapbook back home and how I would love to adorn it with some of those treasures. During those moments of inattention, some of the frothy contents of the bowl would spill out, which I would discreetly wipe away.

I missed the moments of chatter and mischief with my cousins, isolated in my task. They would all suddenly rush off to the three bathrooms in the house to dress in beautiful little dresses made of organdy, with socks and shoes to match. All this was in preparation for the procession, kneeling down on flower-laden streets, following old Father Martin, the French priest, who faithfully refused to return to his homeland.

I was still in the long corridor leading to the kitchen, the storeroom to the right laden with up-country flowers in blue and white, with my gelatine bowl on the table, the contents really snowy by then. Suddenly, I heard a whisper and noticed a movement of precipitation as everyone swarmed out. Even the dogs dashed out. I tried to find out what was happening, but they brushed me aside. I saw my aunts leave as if in procession – the fat ones, the short ones, the plump ones – all with their saris tucked-up to walk faster. I saw my cousins dart out. I even saw my grandmother stumble out with her walking stick, her face strained, her rosary around her neck. The Ammas were silent and would tell me nothing.

It was only when I was much older that I found out what all the commotion had been about. Jonas, the village idiot, who my grandmother took care of, had drowned that day, dragged into the water by his buffalo.

At that time, all those years ago, I had been beating the gelatine so furiously that the bottom of the bowl had given way.

Strange, how Jonas's life had ended even as the bowl had cracked from too much beating.

Strange, how no one had seemed to notice that the bowl was broken.

Journey to Jaffna

UL582 landed at Colombo's Katunayake airport at exactly 7 AM and Geetha stepped down from the plane a few minutes later. Shading her eyes from the sudden glare of the sun, she observed the airport staff going about their daily routine, directing planes to their parking bays, meeting passengers at the foot of the plane, looking a little smug. Behind her, she felt the excitement of some passengers from Italy, coming to the island for the first time; the slim, perfumed, Italian women, the lithe and animatedly gesticulating men, all of them eager for a taste of Paradise. She pressed her palms together to return the farewell greeting of 'ayubowan' softly articulated by the departing crew.

From deep within her, vague memories jostled to the surface, fragments of her life before they had left Jaffna for good. She had been a mere child then, nestling her head against her mother's comfortable shoulder, confronted with the feelings of rejection, surprise and pain, without fully understanding any of it. Padma, her mother, had held her tight, comforting her, a wisp of the soothing fragrance of gingelly oil escaping from her skin. The familiar perfume of jasmine however, was gone forever. They were in a refugee camp, surrounded by ducks, dogs and pigs. Geetha's house had been burnt to ashes, as had her school and worst of all, Appa, her father had disappeared.

It was not easy for her to return now, but she had a purpose.

She got past immigration without a hitch. She helped interpret for a Sri Lankan family from France, a little ruffled by the impatient officer's questioning. She waved away their thanks, but was happy to accept their offer of transport to the capital. While the family looked around the duty-free shops for arriving passengers, she lingered near the music shop. She let her fingers run lightly through the chords of a guitar, remembering someone play the tune, 'Scarlet ribbons.' Music was the core of her existence, of that dormant secret, they knew nothing about back in Italy.

When the family finally emerged from duty-free, happily lugging an oven, a small fridge, a Kenwood beater and a Hoover vacuum cleaner, she joined them to help them get the goods through the customs.

An hour later, she was safely dropped off in Pettah. They seemed ill at ease about leaving her alone there, in the middle of the market, surrounded by baskets of vegetables, stringed red chillies, beaded garlic and dry fish flapping in the wind. She couldn't help resisting a smile at their discomfiture and reassured them that she was quite accustomed to travelling alone. She hopscotched her way through puddles and cracked pavements, looking for the right bus for Wellawatte. She wished to find a place to sleep in the vicinity, close to the bus station.

The first boutique she passed sold strings of jasmine for brides and for pujas. She took a chance and inquired about hostels in the area. The first reaction was one of surprise and wariness.

'A place to stay for the night?' the man in the jasmine shop repeated, spitting out the betel leaves he was chewing, 'where's your husband?'

'Don't have one,' she replied tonelessly.

The man at the neighbouring 'Curry Chambers,' quite taken by her slim and unusual beauty, ignored the jasmine seller's reaction, abandoned his lunch packet and quickly came to her assistance – walk half a mile, turn right towards Sea Lane and ask for Jerry, incharge of the Youth Hostel, he told her. She brought her hand to her chest in a gesture of thanks, the way she had seen Ethiopian refugees do in Italy, and walked away.

The YWCA felt familiar to her, from the woman with a nose-ring sweeping the courtyard, to Jerry, the man-in-charge, who gave away the last available room he had to her. She was somehow at ease even in the dark bathroom with the rusty shower that released hesitant spurts of water, with a toad that kept her company. As if to cool her throbbing forehead, she cupped her hands with water and poured it gently over her head. She let go of the tight control she had kept on herself up to now. She welcomed that invitation to sleep, drew the blinds and went to bed.

Later, she bit into a pattee, a remainder of past Portugese heritage, sort of a local *empanada*. She thanked Gomez for the strong cup of tea, and then set forth on her journey.

Despite her backpack, she walked briskly, ignoring impertinent stares. Thanks to Jerry's instructions, she found the bus station easily. It had to be the right one, with children in colourful attire, the scent of jasmines, women with a red dot on their foreheads. The conductor asked her to take a seat and said he would return the change later. Other passengers flapped about in saris and sarongs, and rushed from seat to seat in sandaled feet. Geetha found a seat next to a kind looking old woman, chewing betel and smiling at her through tiny eyes with a bluish tinge. Sensing there would not be much conversation, she took out her book on Caravaggio and the stolen paintings.

The journey would be from Colombo to Negombo on the coastal belt, onwards to Puttalam and Anuradhapura, before reaching Jaffna.

The bus halted for a comfort stop – restroom visits and a quick bite in a common canteen – usually infested with stray cats who would brush against the travellers' dusty pants and be occasionally rewarded with a piece of fish cutlet.

Then, in Negombo, a group of nuns climbed in, delicately holding their long robes. They were to serve at St Luke's mission in Jaffna. They had bright, enthusiastic faces and each held a rosary, as if to ward off evil. They looked around expectantly, convinced someone would give up their seat for them. Then, a tad disappointed, they stood around till a seat fell empty. Finally, seated all together in one corner, they could be seen making the sign of the cross when the driving became rash now and then. They sang the Angelus to chorus and the driver had to reluctantly lower the volume of the Hindi radio that he kept blaring to stop from falling asleep. The journey was long and Geetha couldn't help counting the miles on the mileposts by the roadside. As the hot afternoon progressed and they headed towards Puttalam, she dozed off.

She was suddenly awakened by someone softly touching her around the neck. She realised, to her dismay, that instead of the old betel-chewing woman, a tall, dark man sat next to her, too close for comfort. His stare was intense and his trousered leg touched hers.

She glanced around, but the bus was too full now for her to change places. Night was approaching and the first corner cafes were illuminated. When the bus stopped occasionally at traffic lights, she peered into the once familiar little boutiques stocked with biscuits, *bulto* sweets, sesame sweets in jars, all treats from her childhood.

The man's face approached hers and she retreated angrily. What could she say or do without attracting everyone's attention?

The stop for dinner was announced near Anuradhapura but she remained immobile. She waited cautiously for her neighbour to get down first. Then she scrambled down the steps of the bus looking around like a hunted deer for a family she could join. She quickly spotted one. They invited her to share their dinner of savoury rice, hot chicken curry and stir-fried potatoes, wrapped together in a banana leaf. Though she was no longer accustomed to using her fingers to eat, it did not stop her from enjoying the meal.

The family asked no questions and she was grateful for that. She didn't belong here, nor did she belong in Italy. They too, were returning to this part of the country for the first time since the war had ended. He had been a professor at Jaffna university till the library he used for his research was burnt down.

She felt for them. Jaffna, the town of her childhood, evoked so many emotions in her; lights over the lagoon where the crab fishing took place, cycling to school in a white school uniform, Karathakolomban mangoes, just picked and served with freshly grated, hot, coconut sambol. If she closed her eyes for a second, she could feel the contours of the fruit, juice squirting all over as she bit into it's flesh. The scent of the fruit from the time it was a young bud, to the ripened fruit in the bowl...little things that Appa could give them, before the war.

They returned to the bus almost reluctantly. She managed to switch places. She realised that by mingling with a family, she attracted less attention. With her hair cut short and her faltering Tamil, she hardly looked like one. Other female passengers wore their hair in plaits, the little red dot on their foreheads signifying that they were married. Then, sleep came over her...things were going smoothly.

It was too dark to see the red earth outside or the palmyrah trees, the fruit of which Appa used for his drink as he laid his worn tennis shoes on the verandah and sat down to enjoy his Sunday drink. She would have so much to tell them back in Italy. But would they listen out of politeness, then look down upon her once she was out of the door?

She shivered slightly despite the heat, almost as if she felt a premonition like she did the night before Appa disappeared. As the bus came to a sudden halt, she spotted a small group of soldiers. Two of them climbed in unannounced for a spot check. They demanded the driver's license, strode unceremoniously through the bus, observing each passenger carefully. Some were asked to alight, including Geetha. The family she had had dinner with did not want her to get down. They were rudely reprimanded; they watched helplessly as she followed the soldiers.

They had noticed her appearance, her western clothes and wanted to know more about her. Could she be a reporter? They asked her to stand aside. Two men questioned her, and a third observed her behaviour. Her throat felt parched, her legs numb, but she would just not show them she was scared. She could feel the silent man observing her, his eyes boring into her back. Then just as she feared, she felt a pressing need. 'I need to use the toilet,' she said a little defiantly, almost enjoying seeing a cloud pass over their impassive faces. They said nothing, but pointed to a tree as if it was the most obvious place to hide behind.

When she returned, they gestured to her to tell her she could go back to the bus. Their attitude was cold, one of indifference. Humiliated, she allowed the tears she had held back to flow, tears of anger and frustration. She did not care who saw them...

At the next checkpoint, the soldiers ignored her. She could sense that her presence had been signalled to them in advance. She could feel their quick, sidelong glances and hear the surreptitious remarks hissed under the breath, almost imperceptible.

The hot sun of Jaffna that blinded them on arrival had warmed the dry red earth. The palmyrah trees stretched out finger-shaped branches in a gesture of welcome. They were home in this deserted land. A thin cow stumbled across in the direction of a well. There were no shops; just ghosts of buildings, a phantom town. A priest appeared on a motorcycle to welcome them. Seeing him, Geetha's eyes opened wide. Could it possibly be Father Pedris, who taught at Sunday school?

Even as he approached, she reflected on why she'd come this far. Wasn't her search one for identity? To get back something she had left behind as a child? Wasn't she nurturing the secret hope that somewhere in Jaffna, her father could still be in a camp? That he was perhaps amnesiac...but still alive?

This priest, if he was indeed Father Pedris, had known her father. They used to sing together. The first lines of his good night song came back to her...'I peeped in to say goodnight.' Her head reeled, her heart throbbed as she contemplated the situation.

Shading her eyes from the glare of the sun, she observed him. She remembered him discussing politics with her father, listening while her father went through the daily ritual of singing Harry Belafonte's 'Scarlet ribbons' to her. The shadow of a long, lean figure fell...Father Pedris was not alone anymore; she could see them both like in a cracked mirror!

She stayed like a bird on a wire, terrified to move in case the image disappeared. It did dissappear, even as she feared.

As she gazed on, wrinkling her eyes unconsiously, she could see just Father Pedris's aged, lined face.

He recognized her. He did not utter a word, but the compassion on his face said everything.

She knew her journey ended there.

Amidst Orchids

'I'm going blind,' she had said, barely looking at him, continuing to tend the orchids in the damp but sunny bathroom. The sunlight found its way in through the fig tree's meshed shadow. It caught the auburn reflections of her hair, brightened her face, dropped down to the silver chain that she so loved and the last beads from which had been ripped off by a baby's grip.

He noticed no tremor in her voice, no fear...just a statement. Her hands came to rest on the orchid leaves. Short nails, he thought, natural, no nail-polish. She wore no rings on her fingers. Just a thin silver band on the fourth finger; a reminder of what he would have liked to forget, but couldn't. Nor could she.

Should he pursue the topic or let it drop? What should the course of action be? He saw her once or twice during the year, caught her voice on the phone for a few seconds once in a while and then forgot her existence, until their next meeting in a crowded place. They knew their roles, what convention and decorum expected from them, and the words would stumble out, 'How are you?'

'Haven't seen you for a long time....'

'How is business?'

'I'd ask for advice,' he heard himself say, cutting the silence short. 'We can research on the subject. It might not be that bad. Maybe you've read too much into what the doctors say.'

'No,' she looked up from the orchids this time and faced him for a second. The intensity of her expression always affected him so much that he couldn't help holding his breath. 'The doctors can't keep the truth from me,' she continued, 'they make me do all these tests every six months – horrible ones at that – the whole routine. Dr Nouari pretends things are under control, but I know how to read between the lines.'

He sighed, feeling helpless. He had never read Shakespeare. He couldn't quote from the sonnets to get closer to her, even momentarily, to comfort her. The firmness in the same serious face and the deep-set eyes, expressionless, devoid of sadness, of all feeling, convinced him that she did know what she was talking about.

She was a thinking person, cheerful and laughing; maybe sad for a while at times, but only until natural optimism and hope got the better of her again. He was a man of a few words, accustomed to getting what he wanted, better at action than at words. He moved with women on a daily basis, charming them, using them, but always kind to them.

She had bathed the orchid plants by then, in the orange pail...a little absent, as if she was walking on a parallel path.

'How crazy,' he thought, 'this Western way of drenching orchid pots in water.' It wouldn't be like that back in Asia where they came from, where orchids grew in their natural surroundings. So much a paradox for someone so natural, to be caught in a system that suited her so little.

Her dress was a legacy of colour, made of natural cotton, slightly crushed as if she'd slept in it. It was neither ironed nor starched, just fluid. 'Suits us,' he thought. The rust-coloured linen shawl on the brown skin was like a reminder of earth. He felt a kind of warmth embrace them both and wanted to approach her, but hesitated. His arms ached from restraining himself, and her breathing revealed that she knew what he was feeling.

'Send me an email,' he said almost gruffly. He didn't want his concern to show. Not his role…he had no part in her life. She didn't want it. He couldn't, anyway. 'Just give me the details. I know most of the specialists back home. I'll get a second opinion from Ajith De Zilva, who's the best there is. We can see him together on your next visit.'

'Yes, let's do that,' she said tonelessly. This time she didn't look up. He knew she had let it drop.

She was up and about again. She would follow her destiny and one day, she would not be able to see him. Nor would she be able to see the person she loved and lived with, anymore.

The Letter

Marie stepped down from the plane. Once again, she set foot on Malaysian soil. They had simplified the formalities for her. The duty free-shops flashed past her on arrival, she did not stop for once. She was just not in the frame of mind for shopping. Martina was waiting for her, holding a board with Marie's name on it.

She went up to her and Martina greeted her warmly. 'You look so much like your Mum, my dear,' she said. Marie nodded unable to speak, holding back her tears for the hundredth time. 'You must be so tired,' Martina continued. 'We'll collect your luggage fast and leave.'

They left the airport in silence. There was traffic on the Malaysian highway and Martina was concentrating on the road ahead of her. Marie recalled that distant stay in her childhood, enjoying meals at night markets, her parents relishing *canai roti* and a hot cup of tea after the spicy food. She remembered their stay in the hotel all together, then her losing a ring near the swimming pool, all four of them watching a movie on an aircrash the evening preceding their flight back to Europe. She remembered treading on the leaves lightly in Bako safari park, in the midst of the rainforest of Borneo, her elder sister leading the way whispering her observations and her fears; was there an iguana in sight? Her mother had hushed them to silence, her hair shoulder length then and caught up in a pony tail. People often said they could be sisters.

The term 'orangutan' provoked a pang of pain, her mother had been fascinated by them. She had gone on about them, read every article in the *National Geographic*, and summoned them for a TV programme on how a group of orangutans actually learned to cook over a stove. 'Incredible!' she said out loud.

Martina glanced at her for a minute. They were now approaching the town of Ipoh. The night workers streamed into restaurants, tourists and locals alike were gazing at aquariums of eel, selecting their dinner.

The strains of Karaoke drifted across from a bar. The transvestites were on their night walks, swaying their hips, handbags on their shoulders. A stray dog darted back and forth, unable to decide between the Chinese and the Indian restaurant.

Marie observed Martina drive. Her parents had mentioned how helpful Martina had been when they first arrived in Malaysia. She pictured them having an evening meal together; her mother picking at her *canai roti* and her father must have ordered his favourite *masala thosai*. The conversation had to be smooth.

She felt their conversation vibrate in her ears, Martina's faint Chinese accent blending with her parent's voices; those voices so often in conversation and also extended in song.

She watched the car take the bend and stop at the traffic lights near the little Indian restaurant where waiters were rushing about and the cook in the corner was making his roti, oblivious to the general commotion, a swirl of smoke curling over his head.

She stopped in front of a small nondescript guest house 'This is where your parents stayed that night,' she said, in a subdued tone. She helped Marie with her luggage. The Indian receptionist who knew her parents, was on duty. He bowed very slightly and said he'd see her upto her room.

She climbed the stairs slowly, picturing her parents before her. From her mother's letter, she knew precisely where the night watchman of that particular floor was seated – the one who shouted 'Happy New Year' every hour before somebody locked him up for the night. Her mother must have climbed the same staircase in her black lace dress, the one she wore for a make-believe New Year's Eve far away from her home. She must have climbed up the steps with her father and they must have stayed up all night, due to the barking dogs and the noisy night workers returning home.

'I hope you don't mind Miss,' the night receptionist broke into her musings. 'We've no other rooms available.' Marie hardly replied, weighed down by the fatigue of the journey and by her own thoughts. She shook her head in what she hoped was a polite gesture. She wandered into the room with the two huge beds. She knew instinctively that her mother would have slept closer to the almirah, her guide book and language books at the bottom of the bed. Her father must have occupied the other bed.

The wardrobe door creaked as she opened it. The black lace dress must have been hanging there in preparation for New Year's Eve. As she stepped down into the bathroom, she could see the wash basin with the broken mirror that they had referred to. She noticed that the washbasin was 'Armitage Shanks,' still another familiar item from her mother's childhood. Her mother had never forgotten her native Asia and was always looking for things to remind her of her first twenty years, those spent in Asia.

'I'll leave you, miss.' The elderly night receptionist Ajith, said. 'Miss Martina will be there to pick you up around 8 AM. Good night, miss.' She responded to his farewell and watched him go down the stairs slowly, his head wearily bent towards the floor. She walked over to the crate of clothes they had left in the corner and rummaged around till she found the black lace dress. She held it against her, inclining her head to a side. A waft of Guerlain perfume floated to her nostrils. Her mother must have turned towards her father laughing, knowing she would find appreciation in his eyes.

Why had they made her come all this way? The identification had been done. She was not really needed. What did the hotel staff know that she did not know? What was it that Martina hesitated to reveal? Her parents were just a couple of mixed origin, often on the move with a collection of business cards, but there wasn't more to it than that. The Chinese owner had clicked with sympathy and offered her a cup of tea. They were usually indifferent to their guests and went about their business, collecting ringgits. The helper who had sung 'Happy New Year' from 9 PM, was now silent. He sat like a puppet, saluting anyone climbing up the stairs to their rooms.

The next day she heard a light knock on the door. 'Miss Martina is here,' came the voice of the night receptionist, not yet off duty. 'She's come to fetch you as arranged.'

'I'll be there,' Marie replied. 'Just give me 5 minutes to get changed.' In less than quarter of an hour she was down. She greeted Martina at the reception and asked her where they were heading to.

'To St Michael's church,' Martina replied. 'That's where I met your parents. Had they not come to the vestry at the same time as me, I would never have met them.' Marie could not help but ponder why Martina stressed the fact. The tinkle of the bells actioned by the alter-boys, announced that Benediction was almost over. The priest was to go on with the wayfarer's blessings. My parents must have knelt for that too, Marie thought.

He bowed over her when Martina was finally able to introduce them. 'I have something for you,' he said in his kind old way, 'She gave it to me before the event.' Marie was filled with anticipation. She tiptoed beside him to the vestry. Martina followed at a safe distance. She observed a dark interior with a table and two chairs. He approached a dark, teak chest of drawers. Taking his time, he opened the bottom drawer. From under a stack of dusty documents, he pulled out a letter quietly. She recognised the handwriting immediately.

'It's for you, from them, before they went,' he said. He placed the letter into her outstretched hands. 'Martina will wait for you outside,' he added, shutting the door on them gently.

Martina sat on the edge of a brown circular bench waiting for her. She remembered taking a photograph of Marie's parents at that same spot. For a minute, it seemed to her that they were standing there beside her. Marie tore open the envelope and the letter fell on the floor. She picked it up, trying to steady herself, to keep a control on herself. Her heart was beating fast.

She just saw what was written at the bottom of the page and took a deep breath. She lifted her head to gaze at Martina, unseeing.

'I'm adopted Martina,' she said, 'she wasn't really my mother.'

'I know,' Martina said quietly, 'I know, dear.'

Traveller's Diary: Laos

On arrival at Bangkok's Suvarnabhumi airport at 12:30 PM and just a few minutes after the jet bridge was deployed, we headed off towards domestic departures. The staff checking the flights for Chiang Rai were raw and inexperienced. They almost tore off the wrong flight coupon of my ticket by mistake. Fortunately I stay very vigilant at airports.

We reached Chiang Rai airport somehow and obtained a list of guesthouses there. A taxi took us to the central bus stand, the departing point for Chiang Khong, the town bordering Laos. The lady conductor advised us to find shelter before dark. We showed our list of accommodation to an approaching trishaw driver and decided jointly to try the first on the list – the Rimini guesthouse, facing the Mekong River. Lizards scuttled along the ceiling as we settled in. The room had a small personal balcony, overlooking the river which formed the Thailand–Laos border.

We wished to cross the river early in the morning and sought the assistance of the hotel owner. Before long, a travel agent was seated on our balcony, talking business. We hardly understood how the fare quoted in travel books of THB 150 became five times as much, but he was to organise everything. Besides, it was far too late in the day to find another travel package! After the travel agent left, I remained on the balcony till late; the familiar scent of cuttlefish stir-fried in the night air brought up pangs of hunger even as late as that.

The next morning, we went in search of fruit for breakfast, while eager dogs were inclined to come and lick our feet. I bought a comb of bananas. The little old Laotian lady handed me back more change than necessary, for the pleasure of doing business.

Rao, the travel agent was a little late to drop us at the Thai border. My boat ticket was accidentally left behind on the Thai side. After a short trip by *pirogue* from Thailand to Laos and thanks to the badges clipped on our T-shirts, we had an escort to welcome us on the other side. We cleared immigration, nervous as we had only one boat ticket for the two of us.

We reported the loss to Rao's Laotian counterpart who checked the information over the cellphone and settled matters. At this point we made acquaintance with our fellow travellers, a sleepy Italian, a lively young American couple taking a gap year in Thailand. We boarded the launch, while waiting for the others. A British traveller demanded a refund as we had been overcharged. For a moment, there was an embarrassed silence!

Six long hours of navigation through the brown waters of the Mekong brought us to the midway point. The voyage was punctuated by an occasional stop, to pick up passengers from neighbouring villages. I had imagined we would travel with the local people, along with their hens and garden produce. Instead, here we were with a bunch of tourists. The younger ones were playing card games with two rather plump Israelis who had since joined in. We struck an immediate friendship with the American students. As the boat reached Pak Beng, the usual touts crept up, with offers of accommodation. Before they even distributed visiting cards, I heard a hoarse whisper offering us a puff of marijuana and we decided to keep a close watch on our luggage.

Night was falling as we took a room at the Villa Salika recommended in the guide book. We sat down to dinner at a place run by a Laotian who was learning French and was happy to welcome us to his modest restaurant. Dinner comprised of a meat dish accompanied by garlic and tomato rice. We returned to our room, refreshed after a quiet stroll. The bamboo balcony was ideal for exercise and ballet practice, as it was far too early to sleep because of the jet lag. At breakfast the next day, we made the acquaintance of some Spanish ladies, who were rather surprised by the Asian fare for breakfast. I opted for fried rice with plenty of basil leaves to last me through the day, as we were unlikely to get anything other than bread and bananas while continuing our voyage down the Mekong river.

The boat ride on the second day was more or less a repetition of that of the first. It was a relief to approach the sleepy town of Luang Prabang. We headed off towards what we supposed to be the town and gratefully accepted the ride of a trishaw driver, hunting for bait for new guest houses. We visited two guest houses that failed to appeal to us and would have continued to search had we not met a young man promoting a family hotel that had just opened. As soon as we visited the Di Nong guest house, (leaving our shoes outside on the veranda as per the local custom) we agreed to move in.

The next morning, we were out in town with no breakfast and no money as we hadn't changed Euros to Laotian Kip as yet. Our first visit was to the bank and then to Laotian Airlines to obtain staff tickets for the domestic sector from Luang Prabang to Vientiene. That visit was of no avail and I had no alternative but to conquer my fear of the local buses. I remembered the wild driving in both Nepal and India. We wandered around aimlessly, visiting stupas and temples. The novice monks were to illuminate boats during the moon festival. They were pretty young in their dark yellow robes and their young sing-song voices revealed their excitement. We kept meeting other travellers from the boat and on their recommendation we stepped in at Miss Lo's unique sandwich house. She produced a luscious dragonfruit and mango drink. Conversing with the owner was a refreshing change. Keeping her voice down, she mentioned the old regime. It seemed that her house and possessions were taken over when communism was at its height. She would sometimes break into French, to express herself better, a tremor in her voice.

Lunch turned out to be a memorable moment, exchanging travel experiences with a sixty-year-old croupier of Austrian-

Dutch origin. There we were, reminiscing about that ever so special feeling at the foot of the Kilimanjaro in Africa. We feasted on steamed rice in rush baskets, meat simmered with coconut milk and tender banana flower, while waiting for the rain to cease in Luang Prabang.

After resting at the guest house before taking a final decision on the mode of travel from Luang Prabang to Vientiane, we proceeded to the night market to take photos and buy gifts. I let myself be tempted by a silver bracelet which in fact turned out to be anything but silver. Old Laotian ladies reached out to say goodbye, I knelt down to embrace them as we finally settled on the 6:30 AM bus the next day. I was not sure I would see them again.

It was our last lazy evening in Luang Prabang and we sat in that dark, little restaurant which was more a menagerie with its unusual decor, a monkey was lulled to sleep by the waitress, an eagle comfortably perched on a post, scrutinised us occasionally. I took good care the cat didn't reach out for my dinner of stir-fried squid. We returned to the guest house, walking through the temple grounds, to start packing after having fixed up the early morning trishaw ride to the bus terminal and the wake-up call.

After a few days in Laos, we learned that no one ever wakes you up at least not in small guest houses, they have trouble waking up themselves. Being a light sleeper I was up at the time we were due to be woken up. I dressed hurriedly and rushed to the reception to check if transport was still available, to find no one there. But the sleepy night guard that I practically shook awake, assured me that everything was in order and we were out before the morning light, picking up our sandals left outside. We were the only tourists on the bus between Luang Prabang and Vientiane. The bus crossed the hills over what seemed like hours. At lunch everything was overpriced. I engaged conversation with a young Israeli travelling with her boyfriend to Vang Vieng. We climbed back into the bus only to return to that same spot half an hour after departure. The driver had actually forgotten a Laotian villager back in the restaurant. Obviously there had been no headcount!

Our first priority on reaching Vientiane, was to find our way to the Thai airline office to check if the flight coupon we had in hand could be exchanged for a Vientiane–Bangkok flight as the distances were the same. However nice and helpful they seemed, they were unable to accept a domestic coupon for international travel between the Laotian capital and the Thai one, which just meant there was no alternative but to cross the border again. This meant practically missing out on the capital city of Vientiane, but we chose to cut short on our trip, to leave promptly, just two weeks after a coup d'état in Thailand.

The second border crossing involved some organisation and the innkeeper really helped greatly. He reached out for his Baygon spray when the mosquitoes and I arrived simultaneously! We asked for a room with a window but inherited a room with a noisy fridge. Darkness fell, even as we ventured out and motorbikes gathered in a cavalcade. It seemed a good idea to have something for dinner before retiring. We looked around, hardly attracted by what was available till we spotted a perfect spring roll parlour, with shrimp and vermicelli and plenty of local leaves and vegetables.

A phone call from Neil McDonald (a local travel agent in touch with us from a distance) briefed us on how to proceed and only the hotel-owner could help us with the impossible task of catching a flight on the other side of the border as early as seven in the morning. We were down at the reception at five am the next morning...the wake up call had actually worked! Our transport had arrived and we were driven to the border in the dark. We were second in the queue and left Laos with no difficulty. They requested 250 kip as departure fees and allowed us to use the little van to cross the Friendship Bridge. It was so packed that we were actually on the footboard.

We were the first out but the last to enter Thailand, being the only passengers required to fill in a form to enter the country. The taxi driver that met us at the Thai border town of Nong Khai sensed our tension. With his smattering of English, he assured us that he would get us to the airport on time. I would rather he kept his head ahead of him instead of turning round to keep us posted on the progress he was making. We made the 7.20 AM flight and were able to board easily. The airport staff apologetically warned us that we probably would not get a meal on board. This happened occasionally to staff travellers and we did not consider this a problem.

On arrival in Thailand's Bangkok airport early morning, we survived hours of waiting by observing the hundreds of mixed-race couples, reading and shopping for gifts till we could finally report for the flight to Colombo close upon midnight. I was contemplating whether or not Francois Bizot's book, *The Gate on Cambodia*, would be a good buy when, suddenly, I heard an all too familiar whisper, the same, it seemed, as when the boat had reached Pakbeng.

I turned on my heels and walked away.

The Waiting Room

I arrived sharp on time for the evening consultation with Doctor L, the surgeon at the Salpêtrière Hospital. The secretary casually informed me that they couldn't find my medical file. Had I by any chance taken it for tests outside or whatever? I replied that no tests had been done outside, no prescription had even been given for such acts. A doubt entered my mind as to the choice of the hospital. How could I even consider an operation if they started out by misplacing my medical record? She finished by retrieving it from a forgotten drawer, however and set my mind at rest.

There were two robed ladies seated in the waiting room. They were engaged in deep conversation and looked up at me with interest. I felt my curiosity stirring seeing them with their Somali style dress and shawl over the head. It took me back to the time my Dad was stationed in Africa that brought up memories of open markets, camel carts before the war started. The older lady tried to engage a conversation, did I know the surgeon? What did I think of him? How had I heard about him? I told her that he had been recommended to me by my physician and that he had an excellent reputation.

She seemed reassured and informed me that they had come all the way from home to meet him. They were staying presently with acquaintances as hotel accommodation was too expensive. I wondered where they were from, the language they spoke between them sounded Arabic and in my mind I tried to place them, remembering the descendants of the caravanners in the Nile valley of Egypt. I remembered those who had called me 'sister' during my sharp negotiation for a green, silk scarf in the Aswan district. As if to put my inner questioning at rest she told me they were from Mauritania and we spoke about the silver jewellery their country was famous for, and which I admired each year at the Paris Trade Fair. She asked me where I was from and I replied that I was born in Sri Lanka where the famous black tea came from.

It was my turn then to meet Dr L and I bade them goodbye. The consultation was brief. I had already decided against any surgery and apparently we were in agreement at least on this matter, saying we could bide our time and decide at a later date should the symptoms recur. Towards the latter part of the consultation an unearthly scream rose in the corridor. I almost jumped out of my seat but Dr L seemed more deaf than usual, he continued to write his notes with the greatest calm. When I asked him if he was expecting someone, he nodded slightly. He commented dryly that the door had not been closed properly.

I got up to close the door excusing myself, wrote out my cheque, asked my usual questions about stress-related cancer and that caused by excess use of soya or sage. He dispelled my fears with his usual placidity, hardly lifting his head while outside, the screaming and ranting went on.

I left the building only to see the Mauritanian lady outside, in an attitude of deep shock. I spoke to her, taking my time as if to help her to emerge from whatever state she was in. She informed me that after I had left she had got a telephone call breaking the sad news that her brother had passed away, back home in Mauritania that very evening.

I didn't know how to react, the situation was so unexpected and after all, we were total strangers to each other.

Right before my eyes she had been transformed from the dignified lady in her flowing Mauritanian robes; there she was rolling on the wet grass in the dark, beating her chest, getting up every few minutes and moaning. I didn't know how close I should get, thinking of an animal in pain; I couldn't gauge her reactions! I decided to forget about getting my number 57 bus to return home. I would stay and help if I could. I imagined the pain or shock one could feel on receiving bad news far away from home and from everything familiar. I knew it could happen to me some day, with my family so far away from here in Paris.

It seemed useless; she was oblivious to all communication, to anything one could say. I asked her if I could contact the people she was staying with, to keep them informed, maybe share the pain, she just did not reply.

Just then, the three attendants who had been hovering around in their white coats, fearing that a patient had been mistreated at the hospital, came out to fetch her, listening quietly to what she had to say. The youngest of them, also of African descent, put her arm around her and guided her back to the hospital.

'Life is never easy.' I heard her say while eyeing me warily, as they closed the door behind me.

Soup Kitchen in Paris

Yet another Monday evening in the 13th district of Paris. We were like those behind the curtain at the theatre, awaiting the cook's signal: ok, ready, let's go!

The whole bunch of us; happy, enthusiastic, leaving our lives outside, our cares behind, to help for just two and a half hours before we, in turn, sat down for dinner to whatever was left.

What's for dinner tonight? Could it be chicken legs or a piece of grilled chicken-sausage perhaps an omelette, maybe even veal chops with green peas, spaghetti, rice or potatoes?

There, they stream in, one by one those from the streets outside, pushing, nudging each other, what's for dinner? They lean forward to see. Soup and soup again! They push the bowl back or ask for more, like Oliver Twist.

'The soup is good here,' some say, 'that's what we come for.' Some are surly, some friendly, some in their Sunday best, some straight from the shower upstairs, slippers on their feet in the thick of winter. Some of them wrinkled and red and reeking of alcohol especially towards the end of the month when they received an allowance from the state, teasing, bullying the others, eager to be the first to be served, to say a few words to the volunteer helpers, the rosy-cheeked American student here, the kind old French lady there. A little old woman walks in, silver-haired and frail, carrying a small bag of provisions with her, no pushing, no pulling, poor and dignified. Polish Pietrov serves her a bowl of vegetable soup and she thanks him gratefully.

The crowd next approaches the cheese and dessert counter, oranges piled to the brim, 'Can I have a second helping of dessert please, as I'm not taking any meat today?' a few minutes to ponder over the question, then the helper agrees and the man is able to wander away with two desserts.

More opt for the same solution, the young American becomes puzzled and needs the queries translated. We tell her what it's about and she agrees after consulting the team leader quickly. The little old woman whose name is Josephine picks up the cheese and hesitates between it and the tempting, ripe, oranges almost falling over the brim. The American student feeling sorry for her, takes a quick look around her and slips a fruit into her hand, Josephine continues her quest discreetly.

The security guards stop the next lot from streaming in, a few minutes for the helpers to exchange a word, share some gossip, tie back their hair, replace the torn plastic glove with another, and push their charlotte caps Marie Antoinette style more firmly on their heads, ready for the next crowd.

A hungrier group come in, red in the face from shoving at one another, anxious that there may not be enough food left – enough soup and especially enough meat. They are fussier people this time:

'I want the sauce on the side,' one say's, 'but not on the right side and not in the center.'

'I want no meat at all,' another adds.

'Is the meat cooked halal style?' a third inquires.

'It's not hot enough,' another one complains.

Not tasty enough for another, for these people from the street.

Josephine gets her first piece of meat for the week and turns to me for the salt and pepper.

I'm at the salt and pepper counter now. 'Two and two' one says. 'Four and four' for another, no salt at all for the next.

'No pepper, only salt,' the one next chimes in.

Then a sharp 'pfeffer' in German, then the Russian with his one eye who I cannot make myself face, is back for pepper for a third time. I even hear a rare word in Spanish, when I don't hear it in Chinese, in Vietnamese or in Arabic. 'We must learn some basic Arabic,' I suggest to my fellow helpers, 'at least words like rabbit and veal and chicken, not useful for pork obviously!'

Romero brings me the salt and pepper left behind on the table, 'I've never given you a present,' he says jokingly, 'accept this at least, it's all I've got.'

It's cold outside and pouring with rain, only around 3 degrees Celsius, they are happy to be here, like at a celebration – only the wine is missing – exchanging words in a rough and tumble way, people who have forgotten what it's like to entertain, to be entertained, to receive or to be received. Clumsy, some grateful, others not.

'Why do you have the TV people in?' one says – the one who comes every day, 'is it to expose our misery?'

'When will the programme be shown?' we ask, clipping our hair back, but there is no reply from those who've come to catch a glimpse of what we see every Monday, just news for them to be exploited on a TV channel, but reality for us, these people known to us that we care for, every Monday. The camera catches Josephine too, as she sits there calm and dignified as if oblivious to what is going on around her.

'There's no bread in the hall,' snaps one of the Directors of the centre, the one always making such reproaches – and Josephine lifts her head abruptly, even as my old, red-faced team leader gets a bread basket ready, I volunteer to take it round the room. He takes over my position of distributing salt and pepper. Round and round the enormous hall I go, often coming face to face with Gwenaelle as if by appointment, to chat for a second. Then we are quickly interrupted by someone putting up his hand for bread. I meet the old lady helper from Brittany too, circling round with cartons of milk. I listen to the ex-parachutist relating his story for the 15th time.

'Yes,' I reply, 'I will try using apple vinegar for cooking meat and seafood.' He's happy, he feels useful. I'm happy too, to see him content. I stop at Josephine's table and she picks up two pieces of bread for her breakfast, which she throws into her bag of provisions.

'Thank you my dear,' she murmurs, 'you're all so good to me.'

'It's a pleasure,' I reply. 'You're so sweet, too.'

I reply mechanically to curious questions on my name-badge. Such an unusual name, where do I come from, how many languages do I speak, do I live here alone, how often do I come here to help, would I be there the following Monday? Josephine doesn't ask such questions; she knows all the replies. She's a little lady who had lost all her possessions, the others had whispered to me when I began my social service, she doesn't talk about herself.

I go next to replace one of the American students leaving early and step in between two elderly helpers, I particularly like one of them, the one whose pilot father had died of a plane crash over Burma and whose husband had died in a factory accident leaving her to look after seven children. The kindness in the aged blue eyes and the now unsteady voice was beyond all measure. She has, in a strange way, adopted me, the one who comes from afar and she reminds me of another person I've always loved and missed. The older helper is now fishing for the turkey kebabs drowning in sauce, I dish out the green beans and a third person pours the sauce over the main dish, on the side, in the middle, on the top according to the person's demands. Josephine has no special requirements, the sauce on top, in the middle, on the side, she'll take it anyway.

Romero has taken over the soup serving now as he often does towards the latter part of the evening, standing nonchalantly, sporting one earring, kind, concerned, a daily appearance, Roberto the cook, takes stock of what's left, brings in sufficient food trays to each helper before it's over and dishes out compliments to all the women not yet in their seventies! He even stops near Josephine. 'Goodnight, my princess,' he says and she smiles a faint, distant smile.

It's almost closing time, the lights grow dimmer, the guard has instructions not to let anyone in anymore, and the night is closing in. You see the wistfulness on their faces as they wander out into the night, for a few a sheltered place to sleep, a temporary abode: for some, a bench, a cardboard box or someone's doormat to sleep on.

Josephine steps out into the night, already absent, absorbed into the hostile world outside, her bag of provisions held tight in her left hand, like a talisman.

From Mogadiscio to Mirissa

We were prepared mentally for the whale-watching trip on the 30th of January 2011, off Mirissa close to the southern point of Sri Lanka, Galle, having read every possible article in the newspapers and magazines. We had left the Point de Gaulle guest-house in the early hours of the morning.

We stepped on to the boat with the fellow passengers of Danish and Chinese origin. Even as I climbed on board I could not help noticing a fellow passenger in a wheelchair and his sharp blue eyes caught mine for just a second. My mind went back to Mogadiscio, summer 1979 and I remembered a British family we had moved with closely. I had just met my future husband then in early May at a Saturday evening party at a British pub evening just before my holiday in Somalia, (my father's duty station), and the one-month revision course in Spanish in Barcelona.

Tom was the 3rd son of the First Secretary of the British Embassy and my younger sister's tennis companion, Peter and Alan being the elder ones, those never to be seen.

Here we were on the boat, my husband and myself.

Tom, (if it was him in a wheelchair – after what I'd imagine to be the British participation in the Iraqi invasion of Kuwait in 1991) with his Cambodian wife and cute, piquant-faced little boy.

The sea was rough and all of us female passengers were fighting against seasickness and there was still not a whale in sight! I engaged a conversation with the Cambodian lady, just the type I like, warm and spontaneous but with a slight reserve, bending one second over her child and then over her husband in his wheelchair. We caught a glimpse of her soul in her generosity.

The Chinese woman was the first to be sick, leaning over the brim, her husband supporting her with one hand, his packets of lemon puffs in the other. I turned away silently so as not to follow suit. After the first fish sandwich (packed carefully by the cook at the small family hotel), I had decided it was best not to eat anything till the boat trip was over and the whales spotted. Now, with the gathering waves, I found it increasingly difficult not to be sick.

Time passed, the colour of the sea, grey since morning, was now turning into an inky blue – almost black. The sea seemed to reflect bowls and bowls of jelly, a parallel to a distant souvenir of sugar rolling over itself in the sugar factory in Gal Oya, a distant memory seen through the eyes of a five-year old child. This image flitted through my mind while the seasickness grew to a pitch and it was my turn to reach for the little red plastic bag I had requested, just in case.

I hesitated between lying down on a bench and staying seated. Water seeped in from one side as I watched, and out from the other side and into the sea. The Danes stuck together just like those in battle and rapped out an order for everyone to put the sliding mattresses back on the benches, the only time that one of them ventured to speak anything other than for Danish!

As my head continued to spin, the disappointed child (the so-called Tom's son) started wailing 'Where's the whale, the whale?' the sound of the child's voice added to my dismay, no whale in sight, the sea-sickness not subsiding and the headache growing stronger.

As if to bring about a change of mood, the young boat boys theatrically signalled the presence of a blue whale in the distance and some of the fellow passengers including my husband, caught a glimpse of its tail before it disappeared! Unfortunately I could not reach the other side of the boat in time. The child had not seen it either so a morose mood prevailed on the boat.

All the Asian women had been sick in turn. First, the Chinese, and Cambodian over the brim, and then me. The water seeping in steadily reminded me of my Dad, then so much younger in Somalia, helping Tom, Peter and the others to bail out the water from a boat off the coast of Mogadiscio. I remember the boys calling the waves 'the biggies' and how insecure we had been, my sister and I, riding that tiny wooden boat in their company!

I thought of my father: then so much stronger and probably during the best period of his life, the comfort of their life in a foreign posting, their close contact with the diplomatic community. I particularly remember the French Ambassador, with a wink in his eye trying his best to pair me off with a would-be diplomat, just out of the prestigious French School of Administration, the ENA.

When the whales finally appeared, it seemed almost an anticlimax, the waiting had been long, the sea fairly rough and hostile, the passengers too sick. When the whales descended on us, all eyes were on them, digital cameras from different parts of the world flashed, Chinese was uttered and so was Danish. The first whale floated gently onto the surface, snorted heavily at the boat to indicate its displeasure. It was followed as if by common agreement by one and still another. Never did they leap and jump like those in the trained circuses of California, never did we actually spot them spouting water, they were just there! They did not in any way acknowledge our presence; we hardly even existed for them.

I floated off into a kind of sleep. The night had been short, the music from the beach party held to close the Galle Literary Festival had kept us from sleeping until very late and besides the night watcher had woken us around five in the morning to catch the tuk-tuk to Mirissa. I let myself be hushed to sleep by the subsiding sea and the feeling of satisfaction of having finally seen the whales in their natural habitat after having followed them around Patagonia, in Argentina and around the coast of Iceland without seeing them.

Sleep came, and I welcomed it. It was stronger than my wish to make acquaintances with the Cambodian wife despite my memories of her country of birth, the town of

Seam Reap near the Angkor site, of setting off to fetch bread barefooted while my family slept, of that country ravaged by war, of Douch, the torturer, and the 300 pages I'd read out to someone and of Pol Pot. I wanted to get to know her, find out what had happened to Tom and everything that had taken place between 1979 when my parents left their posting and now, in January 2011 but no word would come.

The boat had been anchored in Mirissa harbour, we were to say goodbye. I had to know, I felt myself burning with curiosity, I wanted to say, 'Aren't you Tom? Weren't you and your parents in Mogadiscio in 1979?' Instead, I cleared my throat, took on another personality and said in the tone I reserved for passengers, 'What's the next stop on the itinerary? Bentota, Kandy, Nuwara Eliya, Yala – that's good, you'll enjoy it.' Still conscious of his polite, blue-eyed gaze, I hesitated. Should I give him my visiting card, in case we meet again in Singapore where they resided or in the United Kingdom, which they often visited? Instead, I let the matter drop. Reluctantly, I bade them goodbye, closing the chapter behind me.

Rohitha's Cross

I met Rohitha at the ticket counter of the airline that I was working for. He was one of my ex-colleague Rohan's friends, the same type, speaking in colloquial Sinhalese and teasing me about my own lack of fluency in what was my mother tongue.

Time went by and we had lost all trace of each other till one day I heard someone call out my name from a three storey building and it was Rohitha again, there he was cheerfully waving his duster at me. We met, had a chat and agreed to have a cup of tea together on Wednesday mornings on my way to work. He had aged, was tired and had a bad back, though he was cheerful. Grey hairs softened his rather square-shaped face.

Unlike me he was a believer in every religion, he worshiped Sai Baba by breaking a coconut, lit a candle at St Anthony's church in Kochikade, but his strongest belief was in the Cross he gave me, he had actually come across it on his way to work. He swore it had brought him luck and he gave it to me so he could pass on his good luck to me. He told me I was just going through a bad time, and that was part of my fate or 'karma' as they say in the East.

I liked his chatter, his hilarious stories about different employers, those who don't wish their parents to have the best of care, didn't want their toenails trimmed by a healthcare specialist, nor sessions of physiotherapy because it cost too much. He related facts in a simple manner, never passing judgement.

I tried to place myself in the shoes of a person doing a job like his. He knew about the conjugal problems of the couple in the next apartment and warned me not to knock on the wrong door by mistake and to climb the winding, parquet staircase silently. While I continued writing my short stories, he was writing his first novel based on his employers and thinking seriously of directing a film, back home.

It was good to have him prepare a cup of tea or coffee on my way to work for that extra nourishment it brought after still another short night of sleep and before slipping into another day of work. I liked the office he looked after, the jute carpeting, the orchid plants, (one of them which became mine later on, the orange one that blooms in the upstair bathroom) and the silent buzz of inactivity. He introduced me to his rich patroness hoping she would offer me some easy way out to supplement my income when times were tough.

Her puppy would snap at my ankles and run away with my shoes while I endeavoured to keep up a polite appearance.

The promise of work was not kept, but I really didn't mind. Autumn was creeping in and I honestly preferred to return home rather carry my heavy English grammar book around to give private tuition and endure yet another last-minute cancellation as usual when dealing with the rich clientele. Rohitha lost the Wednesday job as the company that employed him suddenly went bankrupt. Now, a large sign hung on the third floor window reading 'To Let' and we lost sight of each other once more. Since he left, I would go past the window. I would look behind as if in expectation, but no one waved a duster at me anymore nor called out my name!

The bluebell bulbs he dropped off at my workplace are now in bloom in the pot outside the house, like the orchids in the upstair bathroom. We have not met for quite some time but browsing through the internet, I learned that his first film had been well received.

I wonder if his copper cross, now safely in my purse, would bring about a change in my luck too!

Rohitha, so artistic, so gifted, had actually jumped off the roof from the building where he used to work and this on the day his film was released.

The Last Day in Colombo

On my last day in Colombo, after listening to the 7 AM morning news, I decided to share a trishaw to drop our Mary (who helps in my parents' home) at church for her confession and then go on to do my shopping at Cargills, for home purchases and for what I was to take back with me. This seemed to me to be the safest mode of transport, after what we had just heard.

I was not really influenced by newspaper articles or headlines at that. My philosophy on life is that wherever I go, I would always return home safely. Mary too had lectured me on where to go and where not to go, but I had laughed off her advice lightly, hardly expecting an explosion at Cargills or a fourth one on the buses, all on the same day.

I enjoy shopping in Colombo, whatever the circumstances and seeing the mix of Asian and European vegetables, small, round, yellowish cauliflower, the long-lined snake gourd and the rough skinned chow-chow, as well as the the sea crabs on ice and the pink cocktail sausages. I stand in line patiently when it's my turn to pay, among impatient executives shopping for their wives and mistresses.

Carrying my numerous purchases, I came out of the shop expecting a queue of trishaws, only to find one sleepy guy waiting for his usual client and who would not budge an inch for me. The other one quoted an exorbitant rupee amount, for such a short distance. I told myself it would do them good to see I was still capable of taking a bus like I did before I left the country. In troubled times, transport seemed to operate less though.

I stepped lightly on the footboard of the approaching bus, managed to enter when someone finally made room for me and waited politely for my turn to pay. I kept getting shooed away at the beginning. I wondered if they wished to be paid for the ride or not. After fraying a path for himself, the conductor finally collected my bus fare and kept telling me to 'go and sit.' Proud of his role, he bullied the passengers into squeezing themselves into corners like sardines. At his insistence, I went and sat but left my groceries at the front of the bus and within the driver's view.

There was a hushed silence. There had been three bomb blasts on buses, that particular day and one would think the passengers were being conducted to Auschwitz. To relax the atmosphere I made a remark or two to the young woman seated next to me. Her eyes like those of her fish, she half whispered her replies to me. Immediately other commuters glared at me for daring to break the sacred silence. Others buried their faces in their newspapers.

It was soon my turn to get down at the bus stop next to the Infirmary. I heard the plain reproaches rising to a crescendo, in troubled times we should know to keep our belongings with us and not scatter them about. They all seemed to be murmuring, talking under their breath.

The bus driver and conductor pointed to my grocery bag and as if by coincidence the driver applied the brakes; the contents fell out and I had a few amused glances thrown at me as I hurried to pick up my things. The driver stared into his mirror keeping a serious face. I just couldn't help wondering if he really had to brake so abruptly as there were no stray dogs in sight. The pot of curd from Cargills broke into bits and the toilet paper bought in a wayside boutique 'Mudalali's kade' tumbled down the steps of the bus and all the way to the entrance of the infirmary much to the astonishment of the patients queuing up to get a number for their consultation since 5 AM.

Lal, the tailor, looked up from his sewing, and Bastien, the launderer, dropped a pile of clothes. The new owner of the 'Appa kade' left his pan of hoppers* and came running to partake of the show.

I retrieved my belongings to the best of my ability, oblivious to the spectators and it was only when I was turning into my lane that I heard the blast and the ground under me shook.

*_Hoppers_ are Sri Lankan savoury pancakes.

The Fallen Angel

She wondered how she could have fallen so low, after years of a middle-class existence, after living in that upstairs house that she had dreamt of, food in the larder, car in the garage, so many clothes to go with the seasons that she kept them stored in three different rooms....The parting had not come easy. Despite years of threats, it was never as simple as that to take that final decision and walk through the door, to know that when she walked through the garden gate, it was forever, there was no coming back. It had been so simple to threaten to leave but so difficult to finally do so.

Their life together had begun when they were mere students. She still was a student and enjoyed everything that went along with that happy existence, preparing for exams, the daily journey on the 67 bus, the chess and ping-pong competitions just out of fun, the occasional Saturday evening party shaking off the advances of the engineer from Orly, or the British rugby player or finding the right reply for the amusing Norwegian's quips.

Life floated from sharing simple meals together, visiting winter markets to buy quail, skating, rock climbing in Fontainebleau, to marriage and its commitments. Suddenly there was no more taking refuge in a university residence when things went wrong. Life had to be faced, had to be lived with what went along with it, weighing the baby every week to check if she was putting on the expected 150 grams, sterilizing six bottles a day, piles of clothes and sheets finding their way from washing machine to dryer. No cinema, no more restaurants. They had given up going to the cinema after that one fruitless effort to sneak the baby in.

She sat in the haunts of the Cité Universitaire the day her mother left, sad and dejected, the harsh understanding that student life was well behind her. The business of real living began to sink into her deeply as she reluctantly left the green grounds. The silence continued when writing her paper with a baby in the play-pen. Fortunately they were able to engage student baby-sitters from time to time and she would sneak off to the cinema to discover the cinema of the 1940s with Moira Shearer, Lauren Bacall and Humphrey Bogart. These actors became as familiar to her as her subject for the Masters' which she had been prompted to choose by Mme Bourcier her course supervisor.

The years passed by, punctuated by diplomas and by birthdays. Friendly neighbours called for a piece of birthday cake and a glass of cider when they were in their second apartment. The woman in the army would come with her two Spaniels. The first years of flat living were a complete change from life in the university residence. The old neighbour would peer through the little slit between the chain and the door, convinced someone was after her meagre fortune. No longer did she feel could she borrow a bowl of sugar or lend some flour in the free and easy atmosphere she had known. Fortunately, the move from a one-roomed flat to a bigger one brought along some helpful acquaintances around her, willing to lend a hand occasionally.

They never agreed about their finances. She was inclined to spend, he was not. She purchased things that pleased her; a pair of shoes, a pair of boots, a dressing-table. He kept all his money for a rainy day, doing his accounts every week.

They argued quite a lot because of the children, did not quite agree on their upbringing. Her life had been like in the army; time for breakfast, time for dinner and time for tea, time for the shower or for the bath and the number of bowls of water before and after soaping herself. He was free and easy with the children. Going out remained a problem but they would use the services of a baby minder to see a film, she remembered with pleasure 'Missing' with Jack Lemmon set in Chile and 'Reds' with Diane Keaton her favourite actress from that period.

Time went on, they moved and knew what it was to be comfortable. They took everyone along, the 2 children, the black cat with the white patch; The same black cat called Minet ran after sheep number 134 in the Pyrenees when they were on holiday. On their return their car broke down on the motorway and after spending a night in Cape Breton, they had to take the train back to Paris with the two children, four bicycles, and the cat in the wicker basket.

They could never sleep in late on a Saturday as the Polish music teacher came in sharp on time with her shrill voice and the neighbours pattered up the stairs to their flats keeping time to Chopin's mazurkas. There was a succession of students to teach the children. One Indian student wrote to her boyfriend during lessons, the American one baked cakes and used up all the flour and the musician helped along with the viola as well and prepared the girls for competitions. The girls learnt both English and French, competed with each other, did ballet and jazz dance, cycled, roller skated with their father, went to the skating rink on Sunday and did everything except go to church.

Their desire to find a place with a patch of green led them for many years to consort with sly estate agents, read advertisements and browse on the internet while saving up every cent and sacrificing their holidays and most forms of entertainment. Their search took them all over the suburbs to flats with terraces and houses with gardens, pursued by inquiring eyes from prospective owners. They returned dejected to their flat, finding nothing to suit their purse within walking distance from the station.

The girls grew up, had boyfriends, got married and left home. They were now free to get about their lives. No more music lessons or getting the girls' teeth straightened or constant visits to the doctor. They were comfortable, there was more money in the till. After a dutiful visit to church they were now free to resume their new life with him on the computer and her switching from one language to another, one activity to another, shiatsu in Paris, ayurveda in Asia, Tai chi in the open air with the eternal bulimia of living. They grew closer, travelled all over, saw the ruins of Angkhor Wat, enjoyed the sun in Corsica and spent Sunday in Florence watching modern ballet with Italian families.

The joy of living separate lives but staying together gave a good feeling. She joined him on his trips to see his aging parents without the reticence she had known in her twenties. Then a change quietly set in with the birth of their first grandchild and from a now carefree couple, they went back to the joy of nappy-changing, heating up bottles, wheeling push chairs and getting to know each of the ducks in the pond with the little one. Suddenly their social life was reduced again and a totally new regime set in. Suddenly it was taken for granted that they were now available for babysitting.

It was somewhat of a joy at the beginning. She would sing Brahm's lullaby holding the baby on one knee and playing the piano with one hand. He inherited the same tasks as 25 years back; heating up bottles, changing nappies. They soothed a somewhat nervous baby and were happy to show him off to their friends. They were the first to have children in their circle. Now they were the first to have grandchildren. Their South American friends came over to share a glass of wine and hold the baby in their arms on the Friday evening wine-and-cheese interludes that she introduced to combine with the initial requests of babysitting.

Then, as the baby grew into a little boy, there was a change of mood. He became capricious, refused his meals like his mother before him, ran round the table to see who could catch him first. Laughingly, he sent peas up in the air, made holes in the salami. He thumped on the piano noisily; only the cuckoo clock would hush him momentarily into silence. He picked strawberries, the ripe and the raw and chuckled as his grandmother dropped ladybirds on his hair.

For a three year old child he was quick to sense the change of mood in adults, and would test their limits of tolerance. He soon shifted his preference from his grandmother, whose voice he responded to and whom he followed with his eyes, to his grandfather whom he could wheedle and coax and who would give in to his emotional blackmail. He would follow his grandfather around and ignore her unless she had chocolate to offer him. He said with his little, piping voice 'It's me who gives the orders!' The atmosphere became heavy and she began to fear the day he was coming over.

Despite her loving the baby, a hostility set in. They were certainly not at loggerheads, but she was not going to give in to the will of a three-year-old child just to please everyone. She thought of her daughter at the same age, such an expert at spitting out carrot soup on her own glasses, painting them orange daily, defying her parents. With the maturity that came with age, she understood it all better. She followed recipes out of the child expert Laurence Pernod's book *How to Bring Up Children*. Maybe it was not the best book.

Compromises had to be made, the couple adapted their routine to suit their daughter's needs. 'Alright, we'll go see *Jane Eyre* another day', they said. 'No problem about the weekly shopping we'll just do it later.' It became like a song they practised and which they now sang in unison or separately. They tried to be as positive as possible. How long do grandparents adapt and compromise?

'How happy you must be,' her elder sister exclaimed with envy, longing to be a grandmother herself. When she watched the aged grandmothers in the park feeding the ducks and swans with small bits of bread, talking baby talk, she told herself that she could never be like that. Her thoughts drifted back to her own childhood, sitting on the fruit tree and picking them delicately before the birds did, a book in one hand, or running to get her swimsuit and enjoy a natural shower at the sight of the beauty of the leaves enhanced by the rain. Then she was eating grapes one by one, still lying in bed after a viral infection following the monsoon rain, reading a book by Rudyard Kipling her father had borrowed from the British Council library. She knew what it was to have influenza over and over again in the dust and the rain.

She was attached to her parents and her sisters. She always loved reading and this made her a solitary person at times; she acquired her vocabulary through reading and also from her father with whom she had studied Greek history. However, her relationship with him was strictly intellectual. She inherited his sense of organisation, his rigour. From her mother she had inherited a certain generosity towards people, a kind of understanding. Now she was an adult and the notions that had been inculcated into her helped her to remain strong. It was this strong sense of duty that kept her from walking away during their first years together, so much a period of adaptation and the biggest challenge in marriage.

As time went on, bitterness and a sense of frustration set in. There was a certain freshness the first time she saw a child crawl, sit, stand, cut its first tooth, utter its first words.

Seeing the early stages of development in a child remained magical, but she was not prepared mentally or physically for everything that went with doing it thirty years after; the late nights, getting up at night because he had wet his bed, persuading a child once again to have his meals or to share her husband's attention and time with him.

Unlike the typical grandmother, she wished to live life fully. She went back at her old university, enjoyed the ease and confidence she lacked during the early years on arrival in Europe. She was particularly attracted to South American music and singing and worked continuously with South American teachers. She took an occasional ballet class feeling no complexes mingling with the younger ones. Being appreciated was something really necessary for her and it had lacked in her early childhood, when she was considered a poor student because she mastered neither arithmetic nor her mother tongue. It came as a shock to her in her last years of high school when the nuns hinted that they expected her to obtain the best results for the school. The change was too hard to handle so she remained an eternal student and nothing was beyond her.

Her eternal curiosity took her through a sprinkling of Russian, of Arabic and Chinese, with a preference for Latin languages. She used words from different languages and would greet people according to her mood and feeling. On Sundays she would only exchange Italian words with her husband for better practice. But her first love was music and dancing and she could see it even in the little one as he tried to move his body in unison with the melody. A kind of misunderstanding built up between her daughter – and herself.

She had grown up to develop the arts and could not adapt to this role not chosen but assigned to her. Her daughter had her own personal problems; difficulties of a career woman engulfed in a world of men, of being sent on business trips during pregnancy and receiving telephone calls from her employers during her maternity leave. With the growing difficulty of making a harmonious blend of her working life and motherhood she could not understand her mother setting days and times for baby-sitting and felt that her mother put her own activities before what she considered a mother's duties.

Obviously, that created a breach in the couple's own harmony. He could spend 24 hours a day looking after children, being the eldest of a brood himself. His bond with this daughter, an intellectual extension of himself, made him particularly understanding and he overlooked both her flaws and her intolerance. The couple started bickering over small things; missed appointments with friends, foregoing an evening at the cinema, the sacrifices that he made and she was not prepared to make. He volunteered to go look after the children while she stayed at home but she was used to having him around, cocooned in their thirty-year-old relationship.

She felt she had to make a choice. She had made a decision in her twenties shortly after her engagement and left everything she was to possess to her parents, so they would be comfortable in later life. Now, she decided that she would leave everything that they had built together behind for him and the children someday. She would abandon their home after thirty years of friendship, the comfort of a warm bed, the staircase on which she had been photographed so many times, the little garden with the strawberry patch under the shade of the fig tree.

She would not see him wake up in the morning, sleepy and absent-minded in his pyjamas, biting a pencil while seated at the computer.

She would not sing for him at the piano that she had proudly bought with her Christmas bonus one year. He would not be there to fix the computer every time it conked off and he would not be there to confide in after a difficult day at work. Nor would he be there to comfort her when she had a nightmare like she did in their early life together, or when she wandered about like a ghost with a bout of insomnia. The decision was not easy to take, but she was so upset by what society expected from her, that she felt it was time she packed up and went away.

So there she sat in the tiny rooftop room, what was commonly called a maid's room in a Haussman style building, sharing the shower with the other tenants and heating her room with a small stove. Her cartons of vitamin milk were on the window-sill, her clothes still in a suitcase and a small crate of apples from his hometown on the floor. She wondered as the events grew fainter in her mind how she could have come to this, what had created this breach, this fall….Her sadness dimming her clarity of vision.

Disappeared from Room 307

'Madam, sorry, she's checked out.'

'I think there must be some mistake. My daughter would never leave for the airport without saying goodbye to me,' the aged voice on the telephone replied.

'Kindly hold on, I've another call coming,' the receptionist turned to his colleague, 'it's a call for Ms Wolinski. What should I say?'

'That she's checked out, obviously.'

'I'm sorry, Madam, Ms Wolinski has checked out.'

'But...that's impossible. I shall hire a driver and come over as soon as I can.' The lady rang off.

The receptionist replaced the receiver and put a paper weight to stop the bills on his desk from flying off in the sea breeze.

The busy seaside hotel on the West coast of Sri Lanka was full at this time of the year.

He reported to the hotel manager that Ms Wolinksi's key had not been turned in on departure. Neither had anyone seen her leave the hotel.

'Start by checking her room at once,' the manager replied.

A green cabin bag was left behind. A toilet case, a vial of perfume and a mild sedative lay on the bedside table. Sea sand trailed between the room door and the bathroom, where a wet swimsuit had been left to dry.

Personal belongings: a bottle of shampoo and a hair brush were strewn on the bathroom floor as if a struggle had taken place.

Downstairs there was a commotion. The waiters and the maids had gathered to exchange the news.

'Which one was it? Was it one of the airline trainees?' one of the waiters asked.

'Was it the Chinese one who got locked out of her room, Miss Jennifer Lee?'

'No, it was the one who usually had breakfast with the trainee from the Middle East. You know, that tall, bearded guy with the intense, dark eyes,' another waiter replied.

'Oh yes, I remember her, the small-made one of Sri Lankan origin with hair down to her shoulders.'

'I remember getting a paracetamol for her when she had a headache,' the youngest of the waiters piped in, 'she gave me a tip for that.'

The manager directed the receptionist to call the airline. He inquired if Miss Wolinski had departed on the flight to Paris.

'So sorry,' the airline staff replied, 'this information is confidential, I'm afraid I cannot help you.'

The manager grabbed the phone from the receptionist 'Please put me on to your supervisor,' he said, rather roughly.

The supervisor spoke calmly, 'I'm so sorry, Sir. As my young colleague just explained to you, we are not allowed to disclose that kind of information.'

Ashan, the taller of the trainees from the Middle East, presently residing in the hotel, stood on the balcony of room 306, engrossed in his thoughts. Just the evening before, the three of them had walked on the beach. The two men had had a bath in the sea and then returned to the hotel pool for a swim, while she stayed at the poolside reading her notes. Ashan had mentioned with some concern that the light was too poor to sit by the poolside, reading.

⚜

The wiry, young nineteen-year-old room boy picked up the handkerchief from just outside Ms Wolinski's door. A whiff of Guerlain perfume floated gently in the air. Would it be a risk to keep it as a souvenir, he wondered. He had knocked on her door that last day to collect the iron, but there had been no response. He had hesitated – should he use his key and enter the room?

The manager entered the hotel with two stern looking police officers, both on the rotund side but one a little taller than the other and with a moustache.

From the balcony, Ashan watched as they walked in and out of her room, followed by the manager and other senior staff.

'We'll be back to speak to each of the staff,' the officers announced as they left the hotel.

Ashan gripped the wooden grille of the balcony with his hands till they changed colour. He hadn't heard her lock her door the previous night. He thought about how he had felt for her the last few days. He had made every effort not to show his feelings for her. He didn't feel exactly at ease about having mentioned her whereabouts to that underground organization because of the pressure they had exerted on him. His roommate came out idly, 'Hey Machan, have you finished looking through the fare break points?' Ashan gestured to him to lower his voice and silenced him with his stern expression.

The manager was at the airport, checking the passenger list with a senior official of the airline. He returned with the certainty that Ms Wolinski had never reported for the flight!

He arrived just in time to see the entire hotel staff being questioned in the staff area downstairs.

'Is all the staff here?' the taller police officer whose name was Wethasinghe inquired of the manager.

The Food and Beverages manager approached the manager and spoke into his ear, 'It appears that the gardener has not reported to work since yesterday and one of the room boys from the third floor has reported sick.' The manager informed the police officers of this.

Police officer Perera jotted the information down in his notebook with a serious air, while officer Wethasinghe addressed the hotel staff.

'I suppose you know why we have gathered here. A hotel guest has disappeared, leaving no trace!' He turned around to see what impact the sentence had made. 'We are here to find out what became of her.'

'Was there anything unusual in her behaviour? She stayed here for five days, I believe?' he asked the waiter.

'No, nothing strange. She came down at 7 AM for breakfast with her notebook. Had the same breakfast everyday – two stringhoppers and a cup of tea.'

'Right,' said officer Wethasinghe gruffly, 'any signs of emotion or tension at the breakfast table?'

'No, she was a little reserved. Thanked us for the farewell dinner. They had seafood from the hotel lagoon,' the Food and Beverages manager said proudly, sticking his chest out just a little.

'Who was she with that evening?' officer Wethasinghe pursued.

'She had dinner with the tall gentleman from the Middle East. Come to think of it, she left suddenly as if she was expecting someone,' answered the manager after some thought.

Officer Perera gestured to the cook.

'Let me think, I was out in the dining hall and I used to explain what was in the salads to her, like the raw pumpkin she had had the evening before.'

'Even on that last evening?'

'No,' replied the cook and the waiter beside him acquiesced. 'She didn't come by the salad bar the last evening....'

⚜

The police returned to the hotel. They rounded up the room boys for questioning this time.

'Do you all know who Ms Wolinski is?' inquired officer Wethasinghe.

'Yes,' said one of the room boys. 'The lady from Room 307. She borrowed the iron everyday and brought it back herself, usually.'

'Even on that last day?' insisted the officer in a deliberate tone.

'No, I didn't see her that last day.' He hesitated before going on, 'You see, Sir, my colleague who has reported sick was on duty on that day.'

Officer Perera then moved towards the pool assistant in charge of handing out bath towels.

'Did you see Ms Wolinski here?'

'No, Sir, only on the day she sat on the pool terrace with the gentlemen.'

'What did you see? Was she often on the cellphone?'

'Nothing out of the ordinary that I can recall, Sir.'

The police officers next approached the man in-charge of transport to and from the training centre.

'Did you see her on that last day?'

'No, Sir.'

'Why didn't you wait for her if she was late?'

'She was the only one to use our transport that day, Sir. The two gentlemen had gone to Colombo. I was due to pick up transit passengers at the airport and run another errand. I would not have left her behind, Sir. A very nice lady she was.'

'That will be all, thank you. Here's my card if you happen to remember anything else.'

Officer Wethasinghe returned to the restaurant area, helped himself to a cup of coffee and approached the head waiter.

'You said she came down at the same time everyday.'

'That is correct.'

'Did you see her every day – Monday, Tuesday, Wednesday, Thursday? Did you see her on Friday as well?'

'I was off-duty on Friday, Sir. You'll have to ask my colleague.'

'Friday morning,' the Food and Beverages manager stroked his chin, 'juice and strong tea…but no, she wasn't down for breakfast on Friday morning. It was Ramazan, Sir. Some of them didn't come down at all.'

'Ok, we're getting somewhere now,' said officer Wethasinghe. 'So, when did you see her last?'

'I saw her last at the farewell dinner. She was due to leave the hotel after breakfast; the farewell gift was on her pillow.'

'How do you know?' snapped the police officer sharply.

'It was reported to me, Sir,' mumbled the Food and Beverages manager with some embarrassment.

Officer Wethasinghe turned to the others, 'We will need to speak to the other trainees, too.'

The Food and Beverages manager rang Ashan's room to advise him of the police officers' visit.

Officer Wethasinghe entered the room first. A slight scent of Guerlain mingled with the humidity of the sea floated in the air. Officer Wethasinghe wrinkled his nose slightly.

'I believe Miss Wolinkski used to pay you visits?' he asked, addressing Ashan.

Ashan avoided his glance. 'Yes, we sometimes revised together.' 'I used to be there, too,' added his roommate, Azan, quickly.

'Is there anything in particular either of you know about this lady?' Wethasinghe asked in a casual tone.

'Nothing in particular, just that she was to return to France just after the final exam,' Ashan replied.

'Was there anything up between you two?' continued officer Wethasinghe, very close to Ashan now.

There was a pause. Ashan shook his head, not speaking.

'Please do not leave the country for the moment,' said the policeman, 'we might need to speak to both of you again.'

They left room 306 and met the hotel manager on the balcony.

'The head waiter spotted the gardener in town and managed to bring him back for questioning,' the hotel manager announced.

'Good,' said officer Wethasinghe, 'bring him to us.'

The gardener came in hesitantly, tugging at his sarong, the receptionist holding him under the elbow.

The questioning began.

'Your name is Loku Banda, I believe?'

The gardener acquiesced, almost inaudibly.

'You do know that a guest from the hotel has disappeared?'

Loku Banda spoke in a resigned tone, keeping his voice very low. 'I do, Sir. I used to trim the hedges under her window.' He gazed at the police officers in deep melancholy, touching his matted hair with his right hand.

Ashan listened from his balcony crushing his cigarette in his hand.

Officer Wethasinghe advanced towards the gardener.

'Did you see her that day?'

Loku Banda gazed at the police officer, fear writ large

on his face.

'Yes, Sir.'

'What exactly did you see?'

While they were speaking, a car drove up to the reception. An elderly lady got out with difficulty, the driver supporting her. The hotel staff gathered at the entrance to greet her.

Loku Banda spoke to the police officer whose attention was focused solely on him.

'She was dressed in a cleaning lady's clothes, came down very early in the morning, her hands behind her back,' he said in a hushed voice, 'and a man followed her closely!'

'Did they see you?' inquired officer Wethasinghe, taking on an urgent tone.

'The man threatened me. He said if I ever talked, he would see to it that I was silenced,' whispered Loku Banda, crouching away.

⚜

That evening, after the guests had retired to bed, Ashan sat up for a long time, sipping a beer outside room 306. Then, he went to sleep as well.

He was in a deep slumber punctuated occasionally by dreams, when the jarring sound of the phone ringing awakened him.

'Hello,' he said, his voice heavy with sleep.

'Hello,' he repeated. He heard someone breathe heavily, then a sort of a commotion. And then he thought he heard her voice!

He sat there, hunched on the bed in his sarong, the receiver still in his hand.

'Ashan?' he heard her say.

He remained motionless, unable to utter a word, unable to move.

'Ashan, are you still there?'

'I managed to travel back to France on my French passport under the name of Villier. The guy from the training centre helped me. You know, the bearded guy...he was with them, too!'

'Ashan?' '...Do you still intend to come here?'

The Lady in the Crimson Shawl

The rehearsal had begun by the time we walked in. The tenors and baritones were clad in blue, the sopranos and the sole alto in green. Carmen, the soprano, in charge of the choir for that concert at the home for the aged was not going to let anything get past: certainly not at less than one hour before the concert. Her expert eyes noticed almost everything: that the pianist's music sheets were not arranged neatly in a folder, that the male singers were not dressed correctly and that the women had not used the appropriate makeup to look pretty and appealing. She persuaded, cajoled and sometimes her voice rose to a stern order rather like that of an army commander. She would snap 'shut up' when the singers retorted, or found excuses for not holding a note!

An announcer, M Vasquez, had been hired for the evening. Outside the concert hall they waited patiently for their turn to be lead in; some in wheelchairs, some leaning on walking sticks and others balancing on walkers. Mr Vasquez paced up and down, speaking in kind, encouraging tones. He had already exerted some pressure on Carmen in the middle of her solo to check if he could bring the throng in as they would not hold out any longer. Could he let them in he asked, at least one by one, had Carmen almost finished the final rehearsal? Knowing Carmen, every detail made the tension increase. She shouted, made reproaches, she altered the choreography at the last minute. 'Let the music sheets fall after the last piece,' she said. 'Be spontaneous!'

They were led in, that audience of elderly men and women. People of many shades of grey. Then there were the ones with blue-tinted hair after a visit to the hairdresser's thanks to that week's pocket money. Some held the nurses' hands, others were wheeled in. Some were enthusiastic, others passive and worn. Some were there only in body, their minds anchored in the distant past.

Mr Vasquez lead them to their seats, kindly, patiently, and handed them a musical tea programme with the names of Mozart, Verdi and Lehar printed on the left side of it. The menu for the special tea-party was shown on the right side – chocolate cake, Pavlova pudding and the French sponge cake – Madeleine with Ceylon tea served out of a teapot. It was to be a grand afternoon, plunging into music for a change while dipping their little French Madeleine into that special afternoon tea.

I sat very still on the third row on the right, hoping I would remain unnoticed, my right hand on my shawl. I observed a woman tenderly touching her husband's cheek, she indulged in a monologue from the opening strains of the concert till the very end. He never reacted. Another one in the same age group swayed to Lehar's waltzes in her wheelchair. She even recognised the strains of the Traviata. I heard her hum with a certain kind of melancholy, a brooding, wishful longing for the past. Two women inmates noticed me, the silent observer, seated from where I could best observe the pianist's fingers fly over the piano, see each singer and truly enjoy Carmen's performance as a prime soprano. I noticed suddenly that the conversation was about me, with the reference to the 'crimson shawl, over the black dress.' 'Who is the lady over there? We do not know her, someone new to the medical staff, maybe? She seems to be by herself?'

They could not possibly know I accompanied the singers. Carmen presented the pieces herself. Her tone had changed from a dominating one to a tender, understanding one. She spoke in almost a confidential tone, as if music was a secret to be shared, some kind of communion between that public so special to her; her own aunt was an inmate of that home for the aged. Her rendering of Violetta's plea to Armando in the Traviata, of Mozart's Aria of the Cherubim and the solo from Lehar's Merry Widow, were her special gift to her aged aunt.

Even before the singing began, as I observed the aged audience, I drew a sharp parallel with school children. They squabbled, pushed their way, some boasted; they knew that kind of music, they said; they had been to that particular concert hall before, Mozart was just an everyday feature in their lives, some said, as regular to them as their wake-up call in the morning!

Others used that moment to confide...one could not possibly trust Mme Raymond, I heard, nor Mme Baptiste.... 'We were three in the room before, now we are just two!' I heard another inmate sigh. 'Be careful of what you say in the presence of Nurse Carpentier, she's always ready with her case of injections!' As for Lucile Boissier, she takes a second helping of teacakes without consideration for anyone else!

The concert was drawing to a close. No one wanted it to end. Those magic moments, so different from the monotony of carrom games, knitting competitions organised by Nurse Carpentier and a then that five-minute permission to go smoke. It was a change from waiting for absent daughters or for a much loved son who'd escaped for an afternoon from the grip of a possessive daughter-in-law! Only one clean-scrubbed adolescent face could be spied in the hall, looking on with affection at his grandmother, remembering the good food she cooked and the jar of sweets on top of the kitchen cupboard, away from his six-year-old reach!

It was the end. To make the magic moment last a little longer, Mr Vasquez waltzed them back to the door, he wheeled the chairs to music, determined to let Lehar's music linger. The woman in front of me asked her husband what he thought of it; he replied with an absent smile.

I wandered out, held the door for the last visitors, and returned a silk scarf to its eighty-year-old owner. She thanked me profusely: had it been a gift from someone special in her life? I wondered....

The squabbling ladies scrambled out, still arguing.

'It was Strauss,' one said.

'No, it was Brahms!' said the other.

The discussion continued. I smiled within myself, content they were still capable of reacting.

Someone else noticed me and nudged her neighbour, 'Look, the lady in the crimson shawl is leaving. I wonder who she is?'

Shrimp Soup

I had always wondered how Grandma Matilda had brought him up, he was so difficult to handle and so strict with us and yet he insisted on the fact that I resembled his mother so much. I had her face, her features and her bones. I had sometimes longed to go away to boarding school, almost regretted that I had wept so hard to get away from going away from home. Once my bags were packed, my little brown suitcase and my night bag with the yellow cotton pyjamas and we were just about ready to go. Only my tears had made him relent and come back on his decision.

Every night before I went to bed, I prayed that I would see her one day; I would actually talk to her, try to understand. I contemplated the bony face in the black and white photograph, looking at us with pity and understanding every time an emotional storm blew up in our house.

I looked at her thin, frail arms and then at mine, the same determined chin that reflected that inner strength to survive our daily battles, the spirit of endurance. I gazed at her daily as if willing her to talk. I stared my silent questions at her and I knew she would reply one day. Alice, who did the housework, used to tell me she felt uneasy when sweeping the upstair living room. 'That lady your grandmother watches me all the time,' she used to tell me. I laughed away her feeling of unease. 'A lovely lady,' my Mum had said. 'You should have known her. She would have been an example to you all.' One day, when I was able to slip a white sari away from a trunk in the storeroom, I draped it around me, pinned an old-fashioned brooch on my shoulder and I looked up at her photo apologetically, 'I've only borrowed it, you can be sure I will put it back. How much I resemble you!' I said. She seemed to smile her little secret smile, a look of approval warming her bony face.

The next day Grandma Matilda was standing at the sideboard while Amme was in the kitchen preparing the food for my grandparents' almsgiving and my mother was busy getting the glasses ready. Suddenly she seemed to be right beside me – her hair in a little bun, the little smile at the corner of her mouth. Putting her finger on her lips so I would stay silent, she pointed out to the little boy playing out in the yard and then I actually saw them; a bunch of children, my father in his blue school shorts, his two sisters walking ahead and he tagging behind. His elder sister turned back to taunt him about something and he retorted. They seemed to be in some kind of argument. He looked far from happy.

One of his sisters dropped her satchel asking him to pick it up. He hesitated and finally reached out for it, reluctantly. His sisters were like tall swaying trees beside him. So there he was a silent little boy with a tortured spirit. His lagging footsteps, lack of joy made him look like an adult disguised in a little boy's clothes.

My mother approached the sideboard, never seeing Grandma Matilda, she brushed past her just feeling her breath for a second, her eyes on the glasses that she was carrying. She inquired whether all Grandma's favourites were ready: the eggplant, the fish, the chicken the way she used to like it? I watched her in silence. 'Mummy,' I whispered but from the preoccupied look on her face I knew then that I was the only one able to see Grandma. My Mum increased the volume of the radio so she could follow the news from where she was, Kuwait had just been invaded by Iraq. I watched Grandma Matilda's eyes widen. I saw her lift her hands towards the ceiling as she heard the news. Then slowly she turned and her gaze returned to the children outside.

'Look – Janis,' she told me and I listened to her for the first time: a kind manner with a mild way of talking. She knows my name I marvelled. They had always told she was very gentle, the opposite of me that way; maybe we only looked like each other; she could have been me in forty years time, I would certainly look the way she does one day, my hair in a bun too.

I followed her gaze, my father in his blue schoolboy shorts had fallen and the children outside in the courtyard were taunting him. I saw a teardrop fall from her eye. I tried to touch her hand a hand, to give it a squeeze, her hand somehow escaped mine 'You see now my child, why he is the way he is, a brilliant child he was, brought all the prizes home, but they' – she lowered her tone mysteriously – 'they were all so jealous; so they all always beat him up.'

'Who are you talking to?' questioned Amme the cook who had just dropped a saucepan almost on Grandma's foot; 'Was I talking then, Amme?' I replied sweetly. She was not taken in. 'Don't you go near the tamarind pot again the way you did last week!' she said threateningly, 'I won't have enough for the shrimp soup. I'll soon have to keep it under lock and key!' How strange, shrimp soup at an almsgiving, this was unknown to my Grandmother and we should normally have had only her favourites, one of Amme's strange notions I would think, in her usual way of ruling the house.

'Shrimp soup,' said my grandmother her voice a little fainter now, almost like one off-stage, 'They certainly didn't turn that out in my time!' And she turned on her heel and walked away, merging into the morning sunlight.

A waft of shrimp soup floated from the kitchen window and lifted itself towards the sky.

Unhooked

There was no one left in the office, or so he thought. The idea of the gym closing up made him sick, yet another autumn evening when he would have to slog while everyone else returned home to their families.

'Sorry to disturb you,' she said in her soft voice. 'If you don't mind, would you please undo this hook. I'm going off for yoga and cannot possibly go in this formal dress that I wore for the sales call.'

'What are you still doing here?' he said, too annoyed at being disturbed to feel any embarrassment.

'Well,' she replied, 'I could hardly finish everything I was supposed to do, and even now I'm running late,' she turned her back towards him. 'Please, I've got to rush.' Her tone was a tad insistent.

He undid the hook absently, still complaining under his breath. 'If you had all these reports to do, you'd have some pity on others. Vanish now and let me get on with my work.'

She ran away laughing, her sports bag swinging from her shoulder. Neither of them realised there was someone else in the office kitchen next door, and it was not the cleaning lady.

The next day there was a strange kind of hush since morning. His secretary brought him the monthly report without looking him in the face. She laid it on the desk with a mild thud and disappeared. He worked hard till lunch time, stopping only for a sandwich enveloped in tinfoil that he had hastily prepared that morning.

The girls were having lunch in the kitchen next door and he heard smothered laughter and hushed voices. Something was definitely going on! When he stepped in to fetch a glass of water, one of the girls deliberately stepped aside to avoid him, pushing her body against the wall, taut like that of a cat in battle. He returned to his office puzzled. The phone rang and he answered it, annoyed that his assistant was not taking the trouble to screen the calls, the way she usually did.

He had an afternoon meeting with the manager and was beginning to wonder if it was only his imagination, or was he really being looked at in an odd manner. People parted in corridors when he walked past and a peculiar aura was palpable; his assistant had called off a meeting without informing him and had not typed the report for the week that had to be presented to the manager; the manager himself had received a personal telephone call during their brief meeting and had asked to be excused. He had left, disappointed and vexed. He crossed the girl whose dress he had unhooked the other night and she flicked her glance away in a flash, as if he did not exist. He did not understand. There were so many unanswered questions and he was beginning to feel somewhat isolated.

The next day she did not report to work and the sniggering and deliberate silence were even more noticeable. He hardly felt like getting up to fetch a glass of water or heating up a cup of coffee as he felt several pairs of eyes bore into his back. The deafening silence cut through him like a knife. When a colleague tapped him on the back with a 'How did you do it?' he knew that the situation had reached its limit, although he still had no idea what was going on. An innocent question on his part was only received with laughter and mockery.

He tried to reach his absent colleague on her cellphone but it soon became obvious that she was avoiding him. He had to know what kind of rumour she had spread!

His annual evaluation was a disaster. He felt that they were pressurising him to leave, pointing out that his sales figures were not good enough. He sat in his office, isolated from the others by his physical position and his mental anguish. In the evening; he tried his colleague's number one more time, but without any success.

The last employees left. Evening greetings and goodbyes in feminine voices rang in the corridor. Then, the usual nocturnal calm fell and he was able to concentrate once more. Around 7 PM, he heard someone turn the key in the door. It was the the cleaning lady, jolly and noisy as ever.

'Oh hell, she's going to make innane conversation again!' he swore under his breath, trying hard to keep his mind on the report he was typing and his eyes fixed on the computer.

She bent and picked up the paper balls that had missed the dustbin, smiling her cheery smile and making the atmosphere a trifle warmer for a fleeting moment.

'How are you, Sir?' she asked. 'Still the last one here? Where is that lady who's around in the evening sometimes, working in her office?'

'She's away,' he replied shortly, hoping she would get the message that he did not wish to talk.

'You should never have gone to unhook her dress, Sir. She tried that with the manager, too,' she said in a casual tone, clicking her tongue with sympathy.

Deftly, she picked up the dust-bin and left his office, dragging the vacuum cleaner behind her, while he stared blankly at her retreating figure.

Nazeem's Prayer

Nazeem got up, opened one eye sleepily. It was late, according to the standards he set himself; time to wash, time for his prayers. Outside, there was complete silence except for regular signals from the pigeons outside, waiting for their daily ration of dried corn.

A little later, he knelt on his prayer mat, piously. The light came in through the flimsy curtain. It revealed a clear blue, wintry sky outside. Pedestrians seemed to tiptoe past noiselessly. It was a Saturday, no cars circulated in that part of the 20th district of Paris. No school children jostled past his window, exchanging sweets, racing each other to the pastry shop. Usually, people tapped on his window pane. He had been in the area a long time; he had become indispensable to them and was a popular figure. Thanks to his infinite patience, the people in that part of the town were able to wear the same shoes over and over again, just a new lace here, a mended heel there, a brand new zip on a boot and sometimes a little bit of bright polish to rejuvenate another pair that had seen better days.

He had taken the precaution of pasting a notice outside, 'Please pick up your shoes before the shop closes for renovations,' it read. Except for those who read no French, the instructions were clear. Almost everyone had come to pick up their precious property: laced boots, platform shoes, Dutch clogs, fluffy boots and even Nike shoes with damaged soles. His shop looked pretty bare.

Someone knocked on his window pane. He was there to collect his shoes. He handed over the receipt dutifully in order to identify his property. When he left, Nazeem turned to the last pair remaining on the shelf. There was no chit of paper attached to the laces, nor was there one inside the shoes. Just a minature sized French flag dangled from one of the laces. He puzzled over it, he who was always so systematic! He pored over his receipt-book, straining to decipher the names and telephone numbers. He tried to visualise each one of his clients. The workmen were due the following Monday. The shop would not open for months....Maybe it would be an idea to keep Maria, his neighbour informed. After all, he was going away to Tunisia. He knew she was in, as he could hear her television on, in time for the news. It was on ever so loud but he dared not comment on it. He noticed that some of the neighbours had started acting strange since the recent events. Those in the flat opposite would turn their heads away, discreetly. Maria had not changed. As always, she continued to offer him a cup of hot coffee.

He read the newspapers lying there from the evening before. Like most people, he knew every scrap of what was going on around him; which heads of state were meeting and where. Their speeches were dinned into his brain. He was familiar with the litany of precautions the public were warned about daily. He could not continue to live in fear though, nor could he anticipate trouble every time he took public transport. Yet, it was not without a sense of relief that he returned to the safety of his one-room flat, his studio after running an errand.

He was not oblivious to the looks of resentment since recent times, even in the bakery where he had queued up for the last twenty years. Sometimes he remembered his native land with nostalgia although he had not grown up there. What future would he have, should he return to Tunisia? Would there be enough shoes to make a living on? An image of donkeys, goats and cactus trees with plenty of spiked fruit floated in his mind for just a second. Impatiently he brushed it aside.

'It makes no sense,' he muttered to himself.

As if something inside him prompted him to go there, he walked with determination to the shoe-shelf. There remained just one solitary pair. He touched the shoes gingerly, willing himself to remember. A little sand spilt on the shelf. He brushed it away gently, in deep thought. Suddenly it came back to him. The boy with auburn hair, Guillaume, who had the habit of tapping on his window as he walked past, his satchel on his thirteen-year-old back. It was the young boy who had plenty of stories to relate about his football matches. He had kindly offered to sell Nazeem a ticket at half price knowing that he could afford no luxury. Now he remembered. Guillaume was to attend the football match at the Stade de France on that bloody Friday, the 13th November! Nazeem remembered his chatter, his enthusiasm and felt a sudden sense of panic. Had Guillaume really gone there or to one of the restaurants attacked that day? And if so, what were the chances of him being alive today?

Nazeem did not know the boy's family nor where they lived. He had left no telephone number or address. For a second, he placed the pair of shoes on the window-ledge – maybe he should do an act of charity and give them away? Wasting no time, the pigeons flew over, anticipating manna in the form of corn!

Then, he held himself back. He cradled the pair of shoes in his arms, feeling helpless, a gnawing pain rising in him. His eyes grew blurry. From far away, he seemed to hear the young voice, still talking, still laughing....

He slumped on the bed... and allowed himself to cry.

About the Author

Chanis Fernando-Boisard was born in Sri Lanka, where she spent her childhood and adolescence. She then went on to Paris to study modern languages at Sorbonne University. During this time, she spent summer vacations with her parents in Mogadiscio, Somalia, where her father had taken up an assignment. She joined American Airlines in 1991, before moving to Sri Lankan Airlines where she was in-charge of group travel until December, 2015.

Chanis won the British Council Short Story Competition in Colombo in 1976 for her story, *The Ayah*, and has written a great many stories since then. During her 26 years in the airline industry, she was able to explore many countries including Borneo, Argentina and Iceland. Her frequent visits back to her home country shaped her sharp sense of observation and sensitivity. She could step back and see Sri Lanka differently, both as a native and as someone who had spent more than half her life away from.

Chanis enjoys learning new languages and is fluent in Sinhala, English, French and Spanish, besides a smattering of Chinese and Portuguese. She plays the Brazilian guitar and sings with a group of 15 musicians.

She lives in Paris with her French husband, Alex, and is the mother of two daughters.